SOUTHERN MAGIC
SWEET TEA WITCH MYSTERIES BOOK ONE

AMY BOYLES

ONE

"I had the craziest dream last night."

I walked into the bathroom wearing my signature Wonder Woman pajamas and Tweety Bird slippers, perfect attire for my twenty-five years. I found my roommate Sarah in her customized monogrammed pajamas like many good Southern gals owned. She ran a brush through her glossy hair.

I caught a quick glance of my crimson and honey hair as I squirted a line of paste on my toothbrush. Brown eyes peeked out from under my fringe of bangs and freckles constellated my nose. "Like, I'm so not kidding. I dreamed there was this guy, he looked kinda like an eighties rock star—black eyeliner, leather, hair teased up, the works. Anyway, he told me I needed to go with him or else."

Sarah shot me a long, lazy glance. "Or else what?"

I scrubbed one side of my teeth before spitting in the basin. "Or else he would have to kill me."

"Freaky," she said without energy.

"I know," I said with way too much enthusiasm. "I mean, I've never been crazy excited to go to work, but I'm definitely glad to not be dreaming about that psycho killer anymore."

For a moment the dream took hold of me. The cold clutch of the man's stare speared my heart. I gritted my teeth and shivered, throwing off the dread that had seeped its way into my bones. Like, freaky seeped into them, y'all.

"Pepper," Sarah said, her voice thin. "Your rent check bounced."

I spat again. "What?"

She shrugged, threw me an innocent smile. "Yeah. It bounced. Listen, this is the third time—"

I raised my hand to stop her. "I'm working today. I'll have the money by the time I come home. I promise."

"I can't keep doing this. Covering for you."

I cringed. "I know. I'm sorry."

She sighed. "Your mail is on the table."

"Thanks," I said weakly.

"Pepper, I'm serious about the rent money."

I nodded. "I know. I gave it to Caleb to deposit. I don't know what happened."

Sarah flipped the ends of her hair. "Maybe that was your problem."

Caleb, my boyfriend of a whopping three months, was supposed to have deposited the cold hard cash I'd given him. My waitressing shift had such weird hours I wasn't always able to make it to the bank during normal operating hours, and I didn't like putting money in the deposit box.

I glanced at my watch. Nine o'clock on a Sunday. No way Caleb was awake so I could call him and find out what the heck had happened to my money. Plus, if I didn't hurry, I'd be late for opening. So I got my butt in gear and headed to work.

I grabbed my mail, which included a padded manila envelope, and walked to my super cool '98 Camry.

The super cool part was a joke.

I filled the radiator to the brim, and I crossed my fingers that it wouldn't overheat on the short drive to Safari Club, the rainforest-themed restaurant where I was waitress extraordinaire.

Well, maybe not extraordinaire, but definitely above average, if I said so myself.

I fired up the engine and drove through the hotter-than-heck

September Nashville streets. I was heading to an awesome job where I served up sweet tea, refilled milk in plastic kid's cups, and magically produced crackers whenever a toddler's lower lip started to tremble—all while grinning ear to ear, or at least faking it until my grin felt reasonably real.

Bob poked his head out of his office. "Pepper, I need to see you."

"Sure thing, boss," I said.

Bob Clements was a total nerd, which made him an awesome restaurant manager—really. With his pocket protector and starched shirts, he was as together as a dessert trifle built out of precisely measured strawberry shortcake layers.

And he was a great shoulder if you ever needed one to cry on. When my father had died of cancer two years ago, Bob's had quickly soaked with my tears. I confided in him, thought of him as an uncle, though we were about as related as a possum and a raccoon.

Bob clasped his hands on the desk between us. "Pepper, you know that on God's green earth, you are like a second daughter to me. Or, a first daughter. Heck, you'd be my only daughter. You know that, right?"

I nodded. "Sure."

He pushed up his nerdy black glasses. "Which is why it hurts me to have to tell you this."

I sat up straighter. What could be so bad that it would hurt his heart? His pocket-protected heart at that.

"Becky said she saw you spit in a table's food."

I gasped. "Never. I would never do that."

Bob shrugged. "Pepper, I know you wouldn't. Problem is, Becky's already taken the complaint to the district manager. The whole thing is out of my hands. Safari Club can't take an accusation like that lightly."

A bead of sweat trickled down the slope of my nose. It dangled from the tip until I wiped it off with the back of my hand. "I would never do that. Becky's got it out for me. Ever since I won the contest to see who could wear the most buttons."

I gestured at my green shirt with the giant parrot stitched on the boob. About a dozen buttons with slogans from *Life's a Beach* to the ever-winning *I Need Vitamin Sea* were splattered all over my clothing.

Bob sighed. "Listen, Pepper. There's nothing I can do. I have to let you go."

Tears swelled in my eyes. Holy crap. This was rent money. This was student loan money. This was all money.

Me, being the optimist, when I entered college, I'd signed up for a major in English Literature, not realizing that a degree in said major didn't qualify me to do squat. And now I owed money for it.

Yeah, I agree, it had been a stupid choice in a degree, with little more than offering me a job as an administrative assistant.

I made more money waiting tables.

Well, not anymore apparently.

Bob patted me awkwardly on the shoulder as way of goodbye. I left his office and headed to my locker to grab my purse. Becky the Liar eyed me as I strode past. I ignored her and grabbed my bag. I slammed the steel door to my locker, but it caught my thumb, sending a jolt of pain radiating up my arm.

"Smooth move," Becky said.

Anger flared in me. Now, being a nice girl, I wasn't prone to saying mean things. *If you can't say anything nice, don't say anything at all*, my father had told me my whole life. So I didn't say anything to Becky—not about how she'd lied, about what an evil person she was, about how I thought she grew horns on her head when people weren't looking.

Nope. I kept my mouth shut and locked my feelings in my chest.

I stuck my throbbing digit in my mouth, grabbed a cup of tap water and headed out past the animatronic gorillas pounding their chests and cheery-eyed kids watching them in awe.

When I reached my car, I popped the hood and poured the cup into the radiator. Last thing I needed was for my Camry to strand me on the side of the road.

Because I was out of a job and had no way to pay for repairs.

My mind raced. What were my options?

I glanced at my watch. It was almost eleven in the morning. Caleb should be up. Maybe I could find out about the rent, weep desperately on his lap about losing my job, about how horrible my life had become in less than an hour.

Sounded like a solid plan.

I slammed the hood. A cat with stiff, gray fur padded on top of my car. I shooed the animal away. "Scat, cat. I'm allergic. Go away."

The animal blinked at me and jumped to the ground. It's not that I don't *like* animals; it's more that I don't care for them.

They just weren't my thing, y'all. They made me sneeze, made my skin erupt into hives, made my throat swell. Let me just put it this way—if hell was a day at the zoo, I'd be stuck there for eternity.

I threw my purse in the seat and cranked the engine. It spat to life. The car rocked as it idled.

I fished my phone from my purse and dialed Caleb's number.

"Hey, babe, what's going on?"

"I just got fired." I held back the tears that threatened to rush from me.

"Oh, babe, that's horrible."

"Yeah." I waited for Caleb to tell me to come over. After all, we'd been dating three months and I was clearly subliminally requesting a shoulder to cry on. This was the time when he needed to be my rock and I could find out about the stuff our relationship was made of.

"Yeah, babe, I'd ask you to come over, but football's going to be on soon and I've got my fantasy team to keep an eye on."

I swear I heard a record scratch somewhere. You know, the kind of scratch that plays in movies when the main character doesn't get the answer they're expecting.

What was that he said?

"So I can't come over?"

"How about we meet up later?"

I nearly yanked my hair from my head. "Sure. I'll come over later."

So I'd been fired for something I didn't do, and my boyfriend didn't give a rat's behind because clearly fantasy football was more important than me.

What else could go wrong with today?

Oh wait. It had already gone wrong.

"Sarah said my check bounced. You deposited the money I gave you, right?"

"Umm...oh sure, I did that. I may not have done it right away, but I did do it."

I groaned. Great. So the check might not clear for another day. What was I supposed to tell Sarah?

A limp, "Thanks," was all I could think to say.

I hung up and headed for the apartment. Sarah was a friend of a friend. The arrangement worked out okay except for today, apparently. She wanted to be a singer, which were a dime a dozen in Nashville, and I wanted to be a, well...I didn't know what I wanted to be yet. I was still trying to figure that out.

But I knew for sure one of the things I didn't want to be was homeless.

My mind whirled on the drive home. I thought about the man in the dream. About his streaming black hair and dark eyes.

I passed an abandoned building, and for a moment I thought I saw him. My head whipped back to look, but nothing was there except a lone newspaper blowing in the wind. I reached my building and slid into an empty spot.

My gaze danced around the car until it landed on the padded envelope.

I crossed my fingers. "Please be a million dollars in large bills."

I crushed it between my hands. "Doesn't feel like cash."

The return address was labeled Magnolia Cove, Alabama.

I'd never heard of such a place.

I ripped open the top, thinking that maybe if it was a million dollars in large bills, I could buy myself a new boyfriend, one who cared.

When I didn't see any money, my hopes crashed and burned. I dug in and pulled out something wrapped in bubble packaging. I tapped it into my palm. A golden key slipped out. A large red stone, one I almost wanted to believe was a ruby, sat fixed in the handle. Curling scrollwork etched the shank. The biting end, the part that got inserted into a lock, was thick and well-worn.

"What the heck is this?"

I reached into the package again and found a slip of paper.

My dear Pepper,

Though we've never met, I've come to understand that you're my one relative able to accept my gift. Keep it safe and it will treat you well.

—Uncle Donovan

UNCLE DONOVAN? I didn't have an uncle named Donovan. Well, that may or may not have been true, actually. My father had told me that my mother died when I was born, but he didn't talk about her family.

And he never mentioned an Uncle Donovan.

"Meow."

My gaze flickered from the package. A gray cat that looked exactly like the one from earlier sat on my hood.

I beeped my horn. "Scat!"

The cat jumped off, and I pushed open the door, dreading the ascent to my apartment.

Sarah would be there. She'd want to know things. Like when I'd be able to pay the rent.

And I wouldn't have answers.

It was all very ugly.

And the worst of it was, I wanted to be responsible. Heck, I didn't want to screw people out of money. I was a good person, one trying her best, but sometimes…

Sometimes life just threw turdballs at you when all you were trying to do was paint freakin' rainbows.

Could someone please just give me a new palette of paint?

Anyway, I dragged myself up the stairs to my apartment. I fiddled with my keys until I found the right one and pressed it into the lock.

Only it wouldn't fit. Or turn. Or do things that it's supposed to—like work.

The knob twisted from the opposite side. Sarah stood in the frame, her big, bulky boyfriend, Bruce, beside her.

A stray red hair fell into my face. I brushed it back and smiled, even though my stomach was souring by the moment. "Something happen to the locks?"

Sarah twirled a strand of curly brown hair around one finger. "Bruce decided he should just move in and take your place. Unless you have the money. Do you?"

I rubbed the back of my neck nervously. "Okay, yeah, about that. I don't."

Sarah glanced at Bruce. He shook his head. "Wish you could stay, Pepper, we do, but it doesn't look like this is gonna work."

I threaded my hands together and brought them to my chest. "Please, I was just fired."

Sarah and Bruce exchanged a glance.

A glance that said that now I definitely wouldn't be able to afford rent.

"Sarah, please. I'll get you the money."

She shook her head. "Sorry. I can't let you in. You've got to find another place to live."

"What about my stuff?" I said.

Sarah puckered her lips into an O. "Once you know where you're going, I'll let you in to move it all out."

My jaw dropped. "What? Where am I supposed to go?"

Bruce pushed forward, blocking my path. "Not our problem. You should've thought of that before your check bounced."

With that the door slammed shut, sealing them inside with my meager belongings.

I'd lost my job, my boyfriend cared more about fantasy football than me and now I was homeless—like, officially.

Oh, had I forgotten to mention that yesterday was my twenty-fifth birthday?

Yep, this year was just looking better and better every moment.

Not. Like at all.

I fisted my hands, trying to shove away the geyser of emotions threatening to surface. I could stay and pound on the door, begging Sarah to let me in, or I could head to my car.

I scuffed my feet all the way down the stairs. Outside sat that darn cat. It licked the tip of its tail. When it saw me, the cat stopped.

It was like the darn thing was waiting for me.

Impossible.

The glass door to the outside screeched as it opened. The cat dodged getting hit, scampering around and out in front of me.

"Scat, cat," I said. "I've already told you I don't like felines. Or dogs. Or any animals in particular."

I rounded the corner to find a man perched atop my car. My knees locked.

It was the man from my dream. The death-metal dude who looked like he was about to croon out some Motley Crue with a pinch of Slash on the side.

I cocked my head and blinked.

He was squatting when I first saw him, but then our eyes speared and he straightened. He wore black from head to foot. His long, ebony hair flowed down his back and he wore clunky silver rings on his fingers and eyeliner rimmed his eyes.

Again, same dude from my dream.

My heart knocked against my ribs.

I opened my mouth to ask him where his band was playing that night and if I could have a free ticket, but then he snapped his fingers. A shimmering blue light flickered atop his hand.

"Pepper Dunn," he said. His voice dripped like velvet smog rolling over a lake.

A chill swept up my back. There was no reason for it to, but something about this guy gave me the heebie-jeebies. "Who wants to know?"

He ignored the question. "You need to come with me."

I quirked a brow. Okay, so I might be a failure when it comes to picking boyfriends, but something told me this guy was trouble, and I mean TROUBLE, all in caps with an exclamation point at the end.

"What if I don't come with you?"

I was afraid to hear him answer, because he'd already proclaimed it in my dream.

He narrowed his gaze. His voice rumbled when he said, "Then you die."

TWO

I backed up. I was not, I repeat, not about to go with this guy.

And coat me with sugar and call me stupid, but I wasn't about to die, either.

He jumped off the car. His feet hit the ground lightly, as if he weighed no more than a feather.

The blue flame flickering atop his fingers grew.

I ran to the right in a feeble attempt to dodge a dude who clearly spent a lot of time playing street magician.

Suddenly the stray cat appeared out of nowhere and jumped on the man's head.

He screamed, throwing the cat off. It landed on its feet. The cat turned to me, and the strangest thing happened.

"Get in the car. Now. He's distracted."

I whirled around. No one was there.

"What are y'all waitin' for? Hurry the heck up!"

I raced to the car, shoved the key in, started the engine and floored it out of the parking lot. My heart thundered against my chest, and my foot shook as I pressed the accelerator. Sweat sprinkled my forehead as I tried to put all the pieces together.

Man. Flame. Voice. Cat.

None of it added up.

My gaze flicked to the rearview. The man stood in the distance for a second; then he started to run. I was so scared, fear lodged in my chest. I wanted him gone, away so he couldn't follow me. Pressure swelled in my gut as I wished for him to disappear.

He vanished.

"He ain't gone for long. He's gonna follow you until you're safe."

I whirled my head around, searching out the voice. There wasn't anyone in the car. "Who said that?"

"Me."

In the passenger seat sat that stupid cat.

"How the heck? What the—"

"Hey, there." The voice distinctly popped in my head, but the animal hadn't moved its lips.

"Did you say that?"

"You see anyone else here talkin'?"

My gaze flicked to the cat. I held my breath for three seconds, and then I screamed. "Ahhhh!"

The cat screamed in my head, too. "Ahhhh!"

Still screaming, I said, "Why are you screaming?"

"Why are you screamin'?" the cat said, still screaming.

"Because you're a cat! You're not supposed to talk!"

The cat threw up its paws. "Ahhh! No one ever told me that!"

I pulled over onto the gravel shoulder. I pressed my forehead against the steering wheel and closed my eyes. "This is not happening. This is not happening. There is not a talking cat sitting next to me, and there was not some faded rock-star illusionist sitting on the roof of my car."

"Oh, there wasn't?" the cat said.

I gulped down another shot of air. "It's just stress. I've had too much stress. By the time I count to ten, the cat will be gone… One, two, three, four, five, six, seven, eight, nine, ten."

I peeked from behind my hand and came face-to-face with whiskers. "Boo," the cat said.

"Ah!" I sat up and wedged my back against the door.

"Sugar, you need to stop screamin'. It ain't goin' to do ya no good. Come on. Rufus is gonna try to catch up with you. We need to get on the road."

I flared out my arms. "No. I've gone crazy. Too much stress. My brain has broken. Today was too much. I mean, you can't lose your job, your home and your boyfriend all in one day."

The cat blinked at me. It pawed its whiskers and said, "Pepper Dunn, you ain't gone crazy. You're a witch and you need help."

"What are you talking about? I'm a witch?"

The cat placed its paws on the dash. "Drive and I'll tell you everythin'. Go. Rufus'll be comin' after ya, sugar."

I gritted my teeth. Clearly I was out of options. I didn't have anywhere to go. When my father died, he hadn't left me anything. I had no other family I knew of, and when I'd moved to Nashville, I'd done it on my own, leaving my college friends behind. Now I wished I hadn't.

The cat's tail flickered. "Get on I-65 and go south."

Well, at least I had a traveling companion, wherever I was going.

"You're only crazy if you don't think you're crazy," I mumbled. "I think I'm crazy, so that must mean I'm sane."

Made sense.

"Right. That's how these things work. I'm not crazy because I realize that I'm not."

"Sugarbear, you need to stop talkin' like that."

Right. And I'm chauffeuring around a cat who likes to refer to me as Sugarbear.

My eyes watered. I glanced at the cat. Fur buzzed around its head. Reaching over, I tapped the glove box button. The door flopped open, and I snatched a handful of napkins from the cubby. I rolled down the window as I felt pressure build inside my sinuses.

"Ahchoo." I sneezed. "Can you sit still for a while? I'm allergic to you."

"That why you don't like animals?" it said.

My gaze slid to one corner. "Among other reasons."

"Well, take an allergy pill. We've got a several-hour drive ahead of us."

I frowned. "To where?"

"To Magnolia Cove, your new home."

I cocked my head. Magnolia Cove. "That's the return address." I fished the package from my purse. The cat scooted out of the way as I dropped the bag on the seat and yanked out the envelope.

"I got this in the mail today."

The cat sniffed the package. "Thank goodness you got it before Rufus came."

"Who *is* that guy?"

"One thing at a time. First things first, you are a witch and you be needin' to come to Magnolia Cove."

"What's Magnolia Cove and what's that key?"

"Sugar, Magnolia Cove is a village for witches."

I smirked. "Why haven't I ever heard of it?"

"Because you weren't a witch before, but you are now."

I blew a wad of snot into the tissue. "What are you talking about?"

The cat blinked at me. "When you turned twenty-five, you came of witch age."

I flared out my hands. "Whoa. Seriously. What are you talking about?"

The cat bit the gear shift as if annoyed. "Sugar, how many times do I have to tell you—you are a witch and I'm takin' you to Magnolia Cove to be with your witch kin. Your momma, may she rest in peace, was a witch. So is your Me-me and all the other women in your family."

I raked my fingers through my hair. In the rearview mirror I caught a flash of crimson. "My Me-me?"

"Grandma, sugar. Grandma. I was sent to make sure you made it to Magnolia Cove safe and sound. Because now that you're twenty-five, Rufus'll want to get his grubby hands on you."

"Who is Rufus?"

The cat's tail twitched. "I'll let someone else tell you about him. The key's in that there bag, right?"

I pulled it out. "This?"

The cat's green eyes sparkled. "You've got it! Praise be to hallelujah! You got the key."

A glint of gold caught my attention. "What's the big deal? Other than the fact that it looks like it's worth a small fortune. Is that a real ruby?"

"Sugar, this key unlocks the most important shop in all of Magnolia Cove. And now it's all yours."

I gulped. My throat had dried from my encounter with Rufus, but now moisture filled it. A shop? All my own? I wouldn't have to wait tables anymore. I could pay my student loans and not go into default. This would be awesome.

"I've never been a business owner. Do you think I can handle it? I mean, is there a massive staff that I have to orchestrate and be in charge of? I've never done that before, but I'm pretty sure I'm up to the challenge."

"Hold on there, sugar. Someone needs to cut back on the caffeine. Just you wait until you see it. You'll love it. There ain't nothin' like Magnolia Cove in all the world."

"And you live there? Wait. Do you have a name?"

"Well, of course I have a name," the cat said. "I'm Matilda Moonpie, but you can call me Mattie."

I bit back a laugh. "Moonpie? You have a last name?"

Mattie nodded. "Course I do, sugar. I ain't one of them old barn cats. I'm well-bred."

"Sure you are."

She dipped her head. "Take this exit."

I jerked the wheel and veered off. My thoughts drifted to Caleb and how much I wanted to call him, tell him about the talking cat, Mattie, but then I figured he'd be chin-deep in fantasy football and wouldn't listen anyway.

Hmm. Maybe I'd call him later?

I followed Mattie's directions down two-lane country roads until I reached a turnoff that didn't look much wider than one lane.

"We're almost there," she said, blinking her green eyes at me. "Just wait until everyone meets you. They're gonna be so excited, I bet they'll pee their pants."

I barked a laugh. I followed the winding road. Giant magnolia trees canopied the drive. They were in full bloom. We passed a sign that read, *Welcome to Magnolia Cove.*

The trees parted, opening up the road. Two- and three-story cottages dotted the landscape. They were painted bright colors with wood crisscrossing over the sides. Cedar shingles graced the roofs, making them look like they were cut straight from a storybook and planted in Alabama.

A bell tower loomed in the distance, and the road became cobblestone. Window boxes overflowing with flowers hung from the windows.

I swear, if my allergies didn't flare and make me miserable, this place would be perfect.

A babbling brook rolled down one side of the hamlet, underneath an old mill. The wheel turned, sending water falling down into a pool where children played.

"Welcome to Magnolia Cove, sugar," Mattie said. "It's the most magical place on earth."

THREE

Mattie directed me toward a shop in the middle of what appeared to be Magnolia Cove's main street. Only it wasn't called Main; instead it was called Bubbling Cauldron Road.

"Here it is. Your store, sugar."

I parked in front of a shop with a dark wooden sign that read Familiar Place. I frowned, unsure what that title meant, but hey, I could at least stay, check it out, and wait for someone to tell me the entire thing had been a dream.

I mean, who shows up and hands someone a key to their own business right as they realize they're broke?

I was waiting for someone to jump out from behind a haystack and say, *Syke!*

I killed the engine and grabbed my purse and key. Mattie jumped out behind me. I had almost reached the door when an older man with a bushy beard and eyebrows thick as my arm raised a hand to me.

He wore slim pants, a vest with a gold watch tucked into a pocket and a top hat.

"You there," he sneered. "Are you the owner of this place?"

Mattie jumped in front of him. "It's hers, Ebenezer. She's got the key fair and square."

I glanced from the cat to the man. He raised a crooked finger at her. "I wasn't talking to you, fish breath. I was talking to the newbie. Does she have the key? Because she can't go in without it. Those are the rules."

I backed up toward the car, feeling very small and insignificant. "I received this," I said, flashing the gold piece.

Ebenezer's fingers twitched. He tapped the tips together almost gleefully. "Oh, that's it. You've got it." He leaned close enough that I could smell the sardine lunch he'd eaten. "If you don't want the store, you tell me, girlie. I own the pawnshop just down the street, there. I'll take it off your hands and give you a fair price."

Mattie wedged between us. "Fair price, my hindquarters. He'll give you a lump of coal for somethin' worth thousands. Now get out of here, you old miser." Mattie reared up, arching her back. "You get out before I call Betty on your head. She won't like you messin' round with her kin."

Ebenezer wiggled his fingers toward me. "You change your mind, you call me." He flashed a business card. He motioned with his finger, and I watched, jaw dropping, as numbers appeared on the white background.

"Holy cow," I said.

"Magic, my dear. You're in Magnolia Cove. Magic all around you," he said. "That's my personal number. You can reach me there anytime." He licked the tip of his finger. "And what's your name?"

"Pepper," I said.

He smiled and traced the card. My name appeared in red ink along with the number. "Call me anytime, day or night. I'm always ready to make a deal."

Ebenezer scurried down the street as Mattie hissed at him. "Horrible man."

"Why don't you like him?" I said.

"He's a Northern transplant. Thinks he's better than us Southerners."

"Maybe you only think that because you're a cat."

Mattie blinked at me. "Sugar, you don't know nothin' 'bout us felines. We're smarter than most of y'all humans. Y'all hang around waitin' for men who aren't interested to call. I ain't got time for that. I'm off catchin' dinner in the time y'all are whinin' about yer love lives."

I gulped. "Okay. You might have a point."

"Now, use that key and see what magic awaits."

I palmed the golden tool. It was heavier than any key I'd ever held before. My stomach fluttered as I stood in front of the double doors.

They were glass, with brown shades pulled down so far I couldn't see inside. I pressed the key into the lock and felt it give.

Snick.

I held my breath and opened the door. Darkness filled the room. I snapped on a light.

Filling the room from one side to the other were—

Animals. Lots of animals.

A floor-to-ceiling cage filled with kittens sat squarely in the center of the store. A bin of puppies sat to the right of the old-fashioned cast-iron cash register. Birds perched in another corner, and the side wall was lined with aquariums stuffed with all sorts of creatures—from water filled with fish to dry-land terrains featuring iguanas, turtles, toads.

The puppies stirred as light filled the room. Kittens yawned, and birds began to squawk.

"What the heck is this?" I said, backing up. "My worst nightmare?"

I did not like animals. I did not. I wasn't crazy about cats, dogs needed too much attention, birds were loud and could swoop on your head, pooping on you without warning, and reptiles were untrustworthy.

Listen, I had watched those shows that feature a person getting eaten by their own large iguana or something. I knew reptiles were really just waiting around to kill their owners.

Untrustworthy, I'll say it again.

Mattie landed on the counter. "Sugar, this is your store."

My gaze flickered to her. "I thought you said it was the most important store in Magnolia Cove."

Mattie's mouth twitched into a smile. "It is. This is the familiar store. Where all witches come to find their animal soul mate."

"Animal soul mate," I murmured, reaching into my purse, hoping to find a tissue. My allergies were acting up, and I could feel the itch of a sneeze just behind my nose.

Pressure built inside my sinuses. My fingers scraped at my purse, but I didn't find a tissue. "Is there a bathroom in here?"

Mattie quirked her tail toward the back. "There."

I raced down an aisle as a giant sneeze expelled from my nose and mouth. A kitten reared up on its hind legs. Another kitten hissed and clawed at me.

Great. They liked me about as much as I liked them.

I found the bathroom and yanked the roll of paper so hard half of it mounded on the floor. Needless to say, that half did not end up anywhere near my nose.

After several huge "ahchoos," I got ahold of myself. I could feel my eyes swelling and the congestion plugging my sinuses.

I exited the bathroom and surveyed the room. I shook my head. "There is no way in high heaven I'm keeping this place. No way."

Mattie paced the counter. "Sugar, of course you're keepin' this place. It's yours. You've got to keep it 'cause there ain't nobody else who can do what you do."

I frowned. "What are you talking about? Anybody can run this store, and they probably wouldn't have an allergy attack just walking in."

Mattie rested on her haunches and kicked out a back leg. "They don't have the power you do."

I tossed the tissue in a wastebasket and fisted my hands on my hips. "And what power would that be?"

The door burst open, smacking a stack of books wedged behind it. Parrots squawked, puppies whimpered and kittens hissed.

"Oh, shut it, the lot of you. If you're not good, I'll cook you up in my cauldron and use you in a spell."

I cringed. I might not be an animal lover, but I sure as heck wasn't going to boil them.

A squat old lady with short silver curls, black sunglasses and wearing a denim bodysuit stepped into the store. A gust of wind fluttered in behind her, whipping the pages of the books and ruffling the birds' feathers.

She plodded in, and the animals ceased all sound. It was like this little lady, who only stood about four-ten, sucked all the air from the room.

The store stilled, the very weight of her personality creating the silence.

She pressed her glasses up on her forehead and stared at me. Bright blue eyes swept me from head to toe and back to head.

"So it's you," she said loudly.

"Me?" I said. "What do you mean?"

"Catch up, kid. You're my granddaughter."

"Your granddaughter?"

The little lady waddled over and didn't stop until an inch separated us. Sheesh. Hadn't someone heard of personal space?

"I'm Betty Craple, pronounced Cray-ple, your mother's mother. Let's get a look at you. Twirl around."

I lurched. "What?"

She butted against me. "You're not deaf, are you? I'm just making sure all your pieces are in the right places."

I backed away. "All my pieces are exactly where they're supposed to be." I nervously tucked a strand of hair behind an ear. This whole situation was making a flock of butterflies kick up a serious tornado in my stomach.

The animals, the talking cat, the bossy old lady—all of it made my throat constrict, my heart race and panic run a marathon through my body.

I backed up toward the door. "Listen, it's been great coming here and meeting you and finding out I've got this *awesome* little pet shop, even if I am nearly asthmatic when it comes to being around animals, but I really don't think this is the place for me."

Now outside, I was slowly pedaling toward my car. "Look, it's been wonderful, but I really don't think this is the place for me... Oh look, a cast-iron skillet is flying all by itself down the street."

It was. A large skillet sailed down the street a little ways, stopped, soared up and circled back down.

I blew out a nervous shot of air. "Wow. You don't see that every day."

Betty's eyes sparkled. "That's what we ride around here instead of brooms. Good old cast-iron skillets, modified of course. You hang around here long enough, kid, and you'll be working magic like that." She tapped a finger to her mouth. "On second thought, by the looks of you, that might not be true."

My hackles stiffened at the insult, and I opened my mouth to say something when that Ebenezer pawnshop guy appeared on the street.

He crooked his back and shuffled over. "Betty Craple. It's so good to see you. Are you convincing your new granddaughter to sell the store to me?"

Anger flashed in Betty's eyes. The old woman raised a fist and hammered it toward him. "Never. She's not selling to you."

He cocked a brow. "Oh? Not even after what happened to Donovan? You're going to make her stay?"

My gaze darted from Betty to Mattie. "What happened to Donovan?"

Ebenezer glided over to me. His caterpillar eyebrows wiggled with what I assumed was excitement. They were so lifelike I wondered if one of them would crawl right off his face and inch away.

"You don't know what happened to him? Why, Donovan—"

Betty butted in between us. "Don't you start, Ebenezer. Don't go around starting rumors."

Ebenezer whirled toward Betty. "My dear, how can it be a rumor if it's true?"

I flared my arms. "How can what be a rumor if it's true?"

Ebenezer thumped the brim of his top hat. "Why, you inherited this shop—a shop you don't have to keep, mind you; one that I'd be perfectly willing to buy with cold hard cash—because your Uncle Donovan was murdered."

I gasped. "That's horrible. Murdered?"

Suddenly cute little Magnolia Cove didn't seem too magical anymore. It seemed filled with evil witches working potions meant to kill.

Okay, so maybe I was getting a little ahead of myself.

Grandma Betty rubbed her forehead. "Ebenezer, you old coot. You stay away from my granddaughter."

He cackled. "Of course, but she may want to know the rest of the story."

I wrung my hands until my knuckles hurt. "What's that?"

Ebenezer's mouth curled into a dreadful smile. "The murderer left a note. It said the new owner would be next."

FOUR

The golden key to the front door of Familiar Place slipped from my fingers and clattered to the ground. "The new owner would be next? No thanks."

I picked up the key and thrust it toward Ebenezer. "You want to buy the place? How much are you willing to pay?"

Betty Crabapple, or whatever the woman's name was, bosomed her way between me and the pawnbroker. "Ebenezer, don't you go scaring my granddaughter. You know perfectly well there wasn't a note."

Ebenezer chewed on some invisible substance. "Well, there might as well have been."

Betty wrapped a hand around my arm. "Come on, kid, let's go meet your family." She took the key from me, locked up the shop and then shook it at him. "You stay away from my granddaughter. She's not selling the shop. It's been in our family for one hundred years, and we're not going to lose it now."

"Speak for yourself," I murmured.

Mattie scampered up as we left Ebenezer on the street. "Don't be afraid," she said into my head. "No one's comin' after you, sugar."

I shook my head. "I don't like the 'died mysteriously' part. Not at all."

Betty turned her head toward me. "You know, Mattie is the only cat I can hear."

I frowned. "She's hopefully the first and only cat I can… Listen, this whole thing has been great. Thank you for introducing yourself to me, but I'm not crazy about animals. They make me sneeze, I get welts when I touch them, I'm highly allergic, not to mention our personalities don't click. Isn't there someone better placed in our family to take over?"

What was I saying? I needed money. I needed a place to live. In one day I'd found myself without anything but the clothes on my back and the purse on my shoulder. Oh, and the cat in my car.

I couldn't afford to feed her. I hoped she was a good hunter.

What was I saying? She wasn't even my cat.

Betty stuffed the key back in my hand. "You're the only one with Donovan's talent. If any of us could take over, we would, kid, trust me. And Ebenezer knows better than to try and swindle you out of it, cause he'll have me to deal with."

She turned back toward him. I twisted my neck and watched as the pawnbroker's coattails flipped up and smacked him on the back. He pivoted around, fisting the air. Betty laughed.

I had to admit, it was funny to watch. I stifled a giggle as Betty clapped me on the back. "See? You're one of us. Laughing at all the right things."

A twinkle winked in her eye, and for the first time in ages I felt the tug of family, and also the spear of pain as I remembered what it was like to lose my father.

I stifled my laugh, pushing it down. "Where are we going?"

We stopped in front of a store that looked like an old-fashioned candy shop. The window display featured candy frogs on sticks, eyeballs in cellophane, chocolate bats suspended from the air. At least I thought they were chocolate.

Betty pushed back her shoulders and said, "We're going to meet your family."

"My family? How many are there?" I said.

She shrugged. "About fifty if you count all the cousins."

I made an X with my arms. "Can you just stop and explain everything? I'm a witch? I can hear cats? What's going on?"

Betty sighed. "It's not a conversation I wanted to have on the street, but might as well." She glanced to the right. "Oh look, there's a sprite. It's going to steal your soul!"

I whipped my head around. "What? A sprite?"

She yanked me up the stairs. "Come on, girlie. If we're quick, we can outrun it."

I didn't see anything, but I was in a strange new world and had no idea if there were sprites that stole people's souls. So I scurried up the steps and into the confection shop.

A bell hooked to the door pealed as we swept inside. The rich smell of chocolate floated through the air. I inhaled deeply, letting the smell soak into my being. Boy, that smell could dissolve even the greatest of worries.

Maybe except for a soul-sucking sprite.

I whipped around and pressed my face to the door. Not one hair or scale of a sprite did I see. Not that I knew what I was looking for, but the faint sound of a chuckle filled my head. Mattie jumped inside the window display.

"Betty lied to me, didn't she?" I said, feeling like an idiot for being such a sucker. "There was no sprite."

Mattie pawed her whiskers. "No sprite, but a very funny witch running into a candy shop."

I smirked at her and then peeked around the store, looking for the woman who called herself my grandmother.

My eyes popped bright at the interior of the shop. Beautiful colorful candies wrapped in crinkly cellophane exploded from every nook and cranny. Sugar magical wands, chocolate witch's hats, licorice broomsticks, and one thing that caught my eye—vibrantly colored jelly beans.

My fingers curled around a small bag.

"Those are witch's beans," Betty said, suddenly popping up beside me.

I threw the bag into the air. "Ah!" I clutched my chest as the candy plopped to the floor. "Don't do that. Don't scare me."

"Aw, you'll get used to it, kid." She blinked smartly. I didn't know her, but a swirl of mischief surrounded her as if she were a little bit of sprite herself. "Now, try those witch's beans. Once you've had those, you'll never go back to any others."

I retrieved the bag. "But I haven't paid for them."

Betty placed two fingers on her lips. "Already paid for." She winked at me. "I've got this one, kid. It's on the house." Her eyes flared. "Try one."

The paper crinkled as I peeled it away. I dipped my hand in and pinched a small red bean between two fingers. It smelled of cinnamon, and when I popped it in my mouth, heat exploded over my tongue, followed by rich, full, crisp cinnamon flavor.

I moaned. "Oh, wow. That's amazing."

"Wait until you try the chocolate ones."

I opened my eyes at the sound of a new voice. My gaze settled behind the counter on a tall woman with caramel-colored hair. She gave me wink and said, "It's naturally red. I keep it this color. My name's Carmen Craple."

"Meet your cousin, Pepper," Betty said.

Carmen rounded the counter and extended a long, lithe hand. "Nice to meet you." Then she wrapped an arm around my shoulders and steered me toward the back. "Everyone's dying to meet you. You don't know how long we've been waiting."

Betty scoffed. "Just her whole life."

I shook my head as I dumbly followed them to the back of the store.

We entered a back door, which opened to a large room set up for a party. A huge WELCOME sign draped the ceiling.

About fifty people yelled, "Surprise!"

I clutched my chest as it felt as if my heart would burst from my rib cage. Smiling faces I'd never seen before all clambered up to me.

Betty pressed me forward even as I tried to wedge back. Man, that old lady had a grip like steel. "Y'all, meet your newest cousin, Pepper Dunn!"

"Pepper, it's wonderful to meet you," said a short blonde with a pixie cut. "I'm your cousin Amelia."

Another blonde with wavy hair down to her butt smiled cheerfully. "And I'm Cordelia. We're first cousins and your first cousin."

"Okay," I said, feeling overwhelmed, underdressed and completely out of my element. Y'all, these folks were in dresses and heels, and here I was in khakis and my Safari Club T-shirt.

Cordelia steered me through the crowd. "The whole town's come out to meet you."

"And eat some cake," Amelia said.

Cordelia flashed her cousin a cool look. "You don't always have to be so honest."

Amelia shrugged. "What am I if not honest? It's true. They love Carmen's cake and her sweets."

Cordelia's mouth trimmed to a thin line. "Yes, but you don't have to ruin it."

Amelia batted her lashes at me. "They came to meet you, too, Pepper."

"But also to eat some cake," I said, laughing. I couldn't help myself; these two were a riot.

"Yeah, it's pretty awesome," Amelia admitted.

A knot of emotions rushed through me. I had never met any of these people before, and here they were welcoming me with open arms.

What if they were psycho killers?

Oh gosh, I hadn't thought of that. What if this whole setup was an elaborate scheme in some sort of evil witch ritual that involved them cutting out my heart while it was still beating and sacrificing me to their horrible god?

I stared at the smiling faces. No sense of dread filled my stomach or flitted in my bowels. I had a pretty good sense of people. I mean, I was a waitress after all—I was used to anticipating what people needed before they even realized it.

Since I didn't sense any ill will, I decided they weren't about to make me part of any ritual sacrifice.

And if they were, I could at least have a taste of cake before I found out.

I met cousin after cousin, redhead after redhead, though there were lots of variations of color—some had blue in their red, dyed obviously, while others had gold and brown crossing their crimson tresses.

As my gaze drifted from face to face and I met person after person, I realized that I looked like these women, and they like me. As much as my crazy conspiracy theory mind wanted to think there was something sinister in all this, the fact of the matter was, these were my kin, part of a family I didn't know anything about.

Cordelia and Amelia pulled me into a corner and offered a plate of cake.

"It's Witch Chocolate," Cordelia said.

Amelia shook her head. "It's actually whatever you want it to be."

My eyes widened. "What do you mean?"

Amelia leaned over, her lips curling into a mischievous smile. "Exactly that. The flavor is whatever you want. For Cordelia, since she's a chocoholic, it's witchy chocolate. For me, it's strawberries and cream. For you, it will be something else. Whatever it is you want."

A simple-looking vanilla cake with white icing sat solidly on my Styrofoam plate.

"What's your favorite flavor?" Cordelia said. "That's what it'll be."

I brought a forkful to my mouth and let the cake slip onto my tongue. At first, tart raspberry drizzled on my tongue, then it changed to a hint of chocolate followed by a trail of vanilla.

"That's amazing," I said. "It's like eating three cakes in one."

Amelia clapped her hands. "See? It's wonderful."

"Yeah," I said in between another bite. "Now I understand why everyone showed up for the cake."

Cordelia laughed. "I like her."

Amelia smiled. "I like her, too." She turned to me. "We might just keep you, Pepper Dunn."

"We loved your mother, too," Amelia said.

I nearly choked. "You knew my mother?"

My cousin smiled. "Yes. Aunt Sassafras was the best. You know Cordelia and I are a few years older than you, so we met her."

Cordelia rubbed my arm. "She was wonderful. Totally unlike our mothers."

I swiped a bit of crumb from my lip. "Your mothers?"

Amelia rolled her eyes. "My mother, Licorice, called Licky, and Cordelia's mom, Mint, are luckily on a cruise around the world. If they were here, they'd be stirring up all kinds of mischief. They think it's fun to be irresponsible and do silly things."

Cordelia nodded. "Yes. Thank your stars they're not here."

I smirked. "They can't be that bad."

Amelia and Cordelia exchanged a glance. Amelia spoke first. "Let's just say that one time they put an itching spell on the visiting football team at the high school game. Tricksters, those two."

Something occurred to me. "Why are most of us women named after food?"

Cordelia threaded her fingers through her hair. "Because Betty is a kitchen witch. Her magic focuses on food. You'll learn about it. Just enjoy the party for now."

"Okay," I said. My gaze drifted around the room until it landed on a man weaving through the crowd. He had shoulder-length brown hair, broad shoulders and a serious scowl on his face.

I nodded toward him. "Who's that?"

Amelia leaned into my ear. "That's Axel Reign, private investigator extraordinaire, and the town's most eligible bachelor."

I quirked my lips in confusion. "Why does he look so angry if he's so eligible?"

Cordelia leaned into my other ear. "Oh, probably because someone just hit on him. He hates that."

I found myself admiring his strong jaw as Axel turned to me. Our gazes met. My throat locked, and a shot of heat coiled around my insides and squeezed. I couldn't breathe. I couldn't even think.

His eyes flickered as if he was trying to read something about me. That slight movement broke the hold. I sucked in air and started coughing.

Amelia tapped my back. "You okay?"

A fit hit me so hard I doubled, nearly falling splat on my head. Way to be cool, Pepper. More like, way to lose a thousand cool points in a nanosecond.

"Seriously," Cordelia said. "Are you okay?"

"Do you think she's allergic?" Amelia said.

"Maybe we need a doctor." Cordelia stood.

I wrapped hand around her birdlike wrist. "No, it's fine. I'm okay. Just something went down the wrong pipe." I knuckled a tear from my eye. "Wind, I think it was."

Amelia slapped my shoulder. "Wind going down the wrong pipe. I love it. But it looked more like Mr. Sexy has a strong effect on you."

"Mr. Sexy?" I said.

Cordelia nodded. "That's what we call him. You two had quite a connection, there."

I scoffed. "I don't know what you're talking about. Besides, I have a boyfriend."

One more interested in fantasy football than my needs.

"Is he a wizard?" Amelia said.

I gave her an are-you-crazy look and chuckled. "No, he's definitely not a wizard."

Speaking of wizards, I took the opportunity to tuck a strand of bright crimson hair behind an ear and glance up underneath a curtain of long bangs.

Mr. Sexy had disappeared. Probably for the best.

Cordelia twirled a strand of honey hair around her finger. "So this boyfriend of yours…are you pretty serious?"

"Yes…I mean, maybe." I grimaced. "I don't know. Caleb's a great guy, but he hasn't asked me to marry him or anything."

I smiled brightly at them.

They both frowned.

Cordelia and Amelia exchanged a look. Amelia cleared her throat. "If Caleb's not a wizard, he can't come here."

My hopes went splat on the floor. "Oh. I'd forgotten about that. Surely there are some exceptions?"

Cordelia shook her head. "No exceptions. Those are the rules."

Mattie the Cat crossed in front of us, and I was instantly reminded of the pet shop I didn't want lurking just down the street.

I gnawed my bottom lip for a moment. "So no outsiders are allowed here?"

"None," Amelia said. "But we're all great. We can keep you company plenty."

I frowned. "So am I trapped here?"

Cordelia shook her head. "No, you can leave at any time. But you can't tell anyone who isn't magical that Magnolia Cove exists. It's only for folks with magic, and it's a pretty busy tourist destination."

Mattie the Cat blinked at me curiously.

"So what happens if I tell someone about this place? You know, someone who's not a witch or wizard or whatever?"

Amelia sighed. "Oh, you wouldn't want to do that."

My brows pinched together. "Why not?"

Cordelia sucked air through her teeth. A whistle bloomed from her mouth. "You tell anyone about this place, and you lose your powers. Forever."

FIVE

What powers? I didn't even know if I had any powers. I could hear a cat in my head, but that might be insanity and not witch powers. This place seemed like a huge joke to me, anyway.

After all I didn't like animals. I'd met one talking cat who I didn't mind too much, but the rest of them?

I hated changing litter boxes, and I knew plenty of people love puppy breath, but it wasn't for me.

Still…maybe I should look in on the animals one more time, make sure all their water bowls were filled and the newspaper changed for the puppies.

And food…they'd need food.

I sighed. Crap. I felt responsible for animals I didn't even really care about.

Not that I'm a heartless city gal, 'cause I'm not. I'm as easygoing as a country girl living in the city could get.

Shucks, I might as well put on Daisy Dukes, cowboy boots, a flannel shirt and call it a day.

Deciding to give the animals one last look before exiting magic town forever, I slipped away from the party and back onto Bubbling

Cauldron Road. The sun was sinking past the buildings, shooting deep shadows over the sleepy hamlet.

I glanced toward the pawnshop. The OPEN sign still flared with light. Good.

As I strode down the street, a flicker caught my attention.

"Hey."

I blinked. Mr. Sexy stood in front of the popped hood of a car. He was glancing over his shoulder at me.

Now, on a good day I liked to think I was attractive, but who the heck feels hot in khakis and a stupid golf shirt with a parrot sewn over the boob?

Pretty sure no one, and if anyone does, well kudos to you on that one.

"Hey," I said in return. I paused, feeling heat creep up my neck as his muscles bulged beneath his shirt.

He rose, wiped a hand on a rag tie-dyed with grease. "Welcome to town. Name's Axel."

I swallowed an ostrich egg in my throat. "I'm Pepper. Thanks for coming."

He flashed a smile. His blue eyes crinkled, and my insides did that weird thing again, the thing that made me feel like I was cheating on Mr. Fantasy Football who hadn't bothered to call me all day.

The air swelled with discomfort—mine, if I had to label who it was coming from. I was seriously not good at talking to men, much less superhot ones.

"Well, great to meet you."

He leaned on the car. "You too."

I speed walked down the sidewalk, hoping to heaven and grits and bacon that he wasn't watching me. When I reached the door, I shoved my hand in my purse, found the key and unlocked the door, not bothering to look back to see if he was watching.

Just kidding.

I popped my head around the open door and saw that Mr. Sexy was not. He was back at work under the hood.

I shut the door. The light switch was still on, though for the first time I noticed the CLOSED sign hung to face outside. I exhaled a deep shot of air from the pit of my gut and braced my back to the door.

Countless hopeful faces of animals stared at me. I glanced at each one and, unsure of what to do, started babbling, because clearly talking to a room of creatures that aren't going to understand one lick of what I was about to say seemed like the best option.

Obviously I was out of said options.

Though sitting down and chowing on ice cream topped with some of those cinnamon-hot jelly beans sounded like the best. Idea. Ever.

Speaking of, I punched my hand into my pocket and pulled out a few, popping them in my mouth. Sweet Jesus-goodness melted on my tongue.

I swallowed and began my pitch.

"Okay, y'all—look, I'm not the owner for you. I don't even like animals. Like, not really. What y'all need is someone who loves you and loves cleaning poop. And smelling poop, and that sure as heck isn't me. Besides, I'm not a small-town sort of girl. I'm a big-city, love-'em-or-leave-'em type."

I shook my head. "That didn't come out right. What I mean is, I'm not the owner for y'all. But don't worry, I'll find one for you."

Then it began. Like a swirl of grape jelly at the bottom of one of those jars where the peanut butter and jelly are mixed—the sounds mingled together like that.

"What is she talking about?"

"Oh, I kinda liked her."

"I was gonna lick her face."

"And smell her butt. You always smell butts—butt smeller."

"I'm not a butt smeller. You are."

"Would all of you shut up. I can't preen my feathers with your stupid chatter."

"Oh, shut it, bird brain."

The entire room erupted in laughter. But none of them were talking. I could hear every single one of them in my head. It was like a symphony of tiny baby voices and squawks.

It was horrible.

I thought being able to hear one cat was bad, but this was like a thousand cat voices on steroids. And the entire time they were meowing and barking and squawking—

I was going crazy.

Surely that was it. Losing everything in one day had cracked me open. I was no longer Pepper Dunn, waitress extraordinaire and person who was occasionally late on the rent money. I was now Pepper Dunn, crazy cat lady who talked to animals and found friends who thought they lived in a magical land where only witches and wizards could exist.

Yeah. I needed to get the heck out of here and sell this key to Ebenezer for a bag of magic beans that would hopefully launch me on a beanstalk that I could ride all the way back to Nashville.

Sounded like a plan to me.

I switched off the light, and all the animals immediately went to sleep. Okay. So maybe when the lights were off, the animals went into some kind of stasis? I didn't know how long my Uncle Donovan had been dead, but as far as I knew, I was the only one with the key who could take care of them.

I locked up and stepped out. Axel was gone, and the sun had slinked deeper down the horizon. A cool breeze kicked up, and I hugged my arms, ready to be done with Magnolia Cove, or Coven, more like.

I reached the pawnshop and opened the door. A bell marked my entrance. I immediately saw Ebenezer off to the side, his back to me. He was hunched over as if in pain.

"Mr. Ebenezer? I came to take you up on that offer to buy the pet shop." I jingled the key even though he couldn't see. "It's all yours."

I could use the money anyway. I'm sure he'd take good care of the animals.

He didn't seem to hear me. Meaning, he remained hunched along the wall. I walked over and tapped his shoulder. "Mr. Ebenezer?"

He whipped around, and it was only then that I saw the knife plunged below his rib cage. He fell toward me, his mouth sagging, the light in his eyes dimming.

I caught the knife in my hand. It released from his muscles and fat, tearing more flesh as it came free in my hands. Warm liquid spread over my hands. Probably blood. Most likely blood. My stomach turned. I didn't want to look down at it. I had a sensitive stomach when it came to these things.

Ebenezer slumped to the floor. I leaned over. "Mr. Ebenezer, are you okay?"

I heard the bell tinkle as someone else entered. It was only then that I realized I was standing over the pawnbroker's dead body, the murder weapon clutched in my bloody fingers.

I looked up, bright-eyed, to see a man I'd never met, a mop of blonde curls hanging in his face. He flipped a badge from his coat pocket. Light glinted off the police shield.

"Don't move. You're under arrest."

SIX

I dropped the knife. It clattered to the floor, sending blood splattering.

"I told you not to move," he yelled.

I raised my hands. "I know. I'm sorry. I'm nervous. I'm new in town and just walked in to sell him the animal shop and I found him walking toward me. He had the knife in his belly—"

The officer showed me his palms. "Stop talking. I haven't read your rights yet."

I stepped toward him, my bloody hands palm up. "But I didn't have anything to do with it. I walked in, and like I said, he was like this big hulking mass about to fall on me and that's when I grabbed the knife—totally by accident, by the way. I do not normally go around grabbing knives and such. Really, I don't. But he practically fell on me and all I was doing was—"

The man rubbed a hand down a tired-looking face. "Ma'am, can you please stop talking? At least for a minute. Long enough for me to call in backup?"

I fisted my hands. They were drying quickly, the blood making them feel thick and sticky. "Yes," I said meekly.

SOUTHERN MAGIC

The door burst open again, and this time Betty Craple, all silver-haired and jean-bodysuit-wearing, crashed inside.

"Toad, what are you doing with my granddaughter?"

The officer's jaw twitched. "It's *Todd*, Betty, and you know it."

Betty's gaze dragged over Ebenezer's body and the growing pool of blood seeping onto the floor around him. I stepped back, not wanting to get blood on my shoes. Look, I didn't need to appear any more guilty than this Officer Todd guy already thought I was.

Betty fisted her hips. "So you finally did it, huh? Killed your uncle so that you could have his pawnshop?"

Todd rolled his eyes and shook his head. "No, Betty, I didn't kill my uncle, but it looks like she did."

Betty snapped the lapels on her jumpsuit. "Who? My granddaughter? Officer Turnkey, you know that can't be true. She just showed up in town. She doesn't have the hate in her heart for your uncle that the rest of the town does."

Todd's eyes nearly popped from his head. "Way to celebrate a dead man, Betty."

Betty crossed to me and curled a hand around my arm. "You're welcome. Now I'm taking my granddaughter home with me."

Todd shook his head. "She's under arrest."

Betty snapped her purse from her shoulder and swatted at him. "The heck she is. Go do your detective stuff and find out the real culprit. It's not her, and I won't let you touch her."

Todd took a step forward. He hesitated. I could tell he was torn between handcuffing me and dealing with my grandmother.

Betty pointed her finger at him. "Remember the time half the town got the purple pimples?"

Todd stopped and glared at Betty. "Yes," he said slowly. "I do. Why?"

Betty sniffed. "Keep walking toward her and you might end up with a bad case of it."

Todd tipped his chin down. From this angle I could make out the sharp jaw and his piercing golden eyes. "Now Betty Craple, are you threatening a man of the law?" He glanced down at his fingers. "Cause

I do declare that if I'm not crazy, then you're threatening me with giving me basically a case of the magical mumps."

Betty sniffed. "I don't threaten."

Todd threw back his head and chuckled. "Then you're plainly stating that if I take in your granddaughter, who has my uncle's blood all over her hands, that I'll definitely get the mumps, which means not only will next Saturday's date night be canceled, but I'll be scratching at my skin, trying to claw off the evil mounds of puss."

Betty shrugged. "You said it. I didn't."

Todd's gaze flashed to me. He clicked his tongue.

Betty chewed her lips. It made her look like a squirrel. "Half this town hated your uncle. If they could avoid selling to him, they would. He was a slum lord of those rickety old apartments on the south end of town—heard they had honey flowing from their faucets instead of water for two whole weeks. Who wants honey when you need water? I'd start checking with them first, but my granddaughter is innocent."

Todd studied me. His golden eyes bored straight to my heart, and I shivered. He flipped his badge closed and sighed. "Okay. She's not officially under arrest, but she's a prime suspect, which means don't leave. You taking her home with you, Betty?"

Betty nodded. "She'll be at the house. We'll keep her here."

I flared my arms. "Wait. Here? I'm not about to stay here. I'm leaving. That's what I was doing when I showed up. I was going to sell the animal store to Ebenezer and be on my way back to Nashville. So if y'all don't mind, that's where I'm going right now."

Todd tucked the badge in his pocket. "Not anymore, you're not. Looks like you're staying in Magnolia Cove."

I quirked a brow. "And if I leave?"

Todd rubbed a hand over his forehead as if to say *why me?* "If you leave, we will track you down, arrest you and bring you back to here, where you'll be tried by a council of witches." He paused, took a hard step toward me. "And let me assure you, witches don't look kindly on other witches who flee."

I gulped. "Which means?"

"They'll find you guilty," he said, his voice so rough it turned into a growl.

"And if I'm found guilty?" I said.

Betty took my arm. "It's a nasty punishment. Worse than the magical mumps. You get sent to a magical prison. It's buried deep in the earth, under an old system of caves. No light, no contact with people. Most go mad."

I grimaced. "Sounds horrible. What's it called?"

Betty's voice grew spooky. "Witcheroo."

I frowned. "Witcheroo? It sounds more like a crazy caper than a prison."

Todd's eyes narrowed. "Trust me. It's very serious, and unless you want to wind up one of its inmates plagued by insanity, I suggest you stay in Magnolia Cove until this entire thing is cleared up."

Okay. Well, I guess he told me.

A slew of police officers—I suppose they were police officers because they all wore badges like Ranger Todd—showed up. They weren't in plainclothes. Instead they all wore big cowboy hats, handkerchiefs and dusters.

They looked kinda like Hugh Jackman in *Van Helsing*. I didn't have the heart to tell to them that it wasn't a very good movie and that they'd do better to dress closer to Neo from *The Matrix*.

Anyway, I explained what happened with Ebenezer, and about an hour later I was following Betty through downtown Magnolia Cove to a copse of houses a few streets behind downtown.

One looked exactly like a decorated gingerbread house with swirling candies, gumdrops stuck to the roof and even icing window shutters.

"Whose house is that?" I said.

"It's Carmen's. Neat, huh?"

I nodded. "Yes, very." As we strode past, a whisper of mint drifted up my nose. "Actually, that is cool. Is it real?"

Betty nodded. "Yep. Go grab a bite. Sometimes local children do and Carmen replaces it. It's spelled to stay clean and free of germs."

"Well, okay," I said. "You know, I don't know anything about this whole witchy stuff. I feel like I've been thrown into an ocean and told to sink or swim."

Betty shot me a sympathetic look. "Let's get you in, get you a glass of sweet tea and some cornbread and we'll discuss everything. Your cousins will be there, too, Cordelia and Amelia—they live with me."

"Oh, that's good." I guessed. Heck, at this point I didn't know my butthole from my navel. On top of all the craziness in the past day, I was now accused of murder.

Awesome.

Betty led me through a picket fence to a neat little white cottage with red shutters and a creeping vine winding over the door.

I stepped up on the porch. The vine twisted from the wall. A bud that looked more Venus flytrap than innocent rose shot out and wrapped around my arm.

"Let her go, Jennie," Betty snapped. "She's family."

The vine sagged as if whimpering and slowly unwound from my wrist. The bud sniffed around my head and retreated back to Betty. She patted it like a dog.

Well, if that wasn't magic, I didn't know what was.

"Jennie protects the house. Attacks anyone she doesn't know."

"Sounds like a perfect guard-vine," I said.

Betty smiled. "That's exactly what she is. You are a witch, you know."

I ducked under the vine as Betty opened the door. "Other than the fact that I can hear animals, I'm not convinced that I can work magic."

We stepped inside. The cottage was cheery, bright with cream walls. A cozy fire crackled in the hearth even though it was summer, sconces cast amber light and lace doilies covered almost every available surface.

There were also pictures everywhere, framed colorfully in borders of reds, yellows and blues. Herbs hung drying on the walls and across the mantle. I peeked into the fire and noticed a cauldron bubbling away happily. I sniffed. Smelled of stew. Betty snapped her fingers, and a cast-iron skillet appeared above the licking flames.

"Holy crap," I said.

"You'll get used to the magic. For some it takes longer than others."

Yellow batter filled the skillet to the brim, though it was quickly hardening and turning gold.

"Cornbread," I said.

Betty smiled. "Made with Crisco. Only the best for us witches."

I smiled. I stood awkwardly in the room until Betty motioned for me to sit. I lowered myself onto the overstuffed couch. I leaned on one arm and found myself crushing a delicate doily. I sat up, grimacing.

Betty waved dismissively. "It'll be fine. It's only a doily. I can fix it with magic."

I cracked my knuckles nervously. "Yeah, so about this whole magic thing. Can you please explain it? I don't understand anything that's going on."

Betty shook her head. "It's a shame you were brought in this way. It's not what we wanted for you. You should've known us—all of us—but your mother dying in childbirth messed all that up."

I raked my fingers through my hair. "What does that mean?"

Betty flicked a hand, and a service of iced tea appeared. With another flick, a glass popped right in front of me.

I threw up my hands. "Ah!"

Betty shrugged. "Sorry. I forget that folks don't know what it's like to be around magic."

I curled my fingers around the chilled glass. "It's okay." I sipped the brown liquid. Sugared goodness slipped over my tongue and down my throat. Deciding a bit more sugar couldn't hurt, I grabbed a handful of jelly beans and added them to the mix.

I sighed as the flavors of lemon and strawberry mixed with the tea. "Thank you. I needed this. So tell me everything."

Betty tugged her silvery curls. The curls pulled off, revealing a bald pate beneath. "Sorry. The wig itches. I've been working on creating one that doesn't, but so far it hasn't worked out."

I tried to hide my fright at her baldness—the smooth skin, the few liver spots decorating it—but I'm not sure I succeeded.

"Your father didn't want to have anything to do with the witch side of the family," she said. "When your mother, my beautiful Sassafras, died, he was offered a choice—allow us into your life or not. He chose the latter. A regular witch's powers come in when a person's a teenager, if they're around magic. Since you weren't, they didn't flare until now—when you turned twenty-five. At the same time, your uncle died, leaving you the store—which is now yours to run.

"We sent Mattie to find you. She's brilliant when it comes to tracking."

I felt a thin body tangle around my legs. I glanced down and saw the cat blink up at me. Against my better judgment, I stroked her head until a rolling purr curled from her throat.

"She's a nice cat," I said, "but I don't understand how I'm the only person who can run the familiar shop. Aren't there others?"

Betty shook her glass of tea until the ice clinked up the sides. "Oh no. You see, only very special witches can hear animals. Donovan had the gift, then your mother, which meant you would also have it—or at least we hoped, since he died so untimely."

I blinked at her. "Yes. I'd forgotten all about that. Did someone kill Donovan?"

Betty smoothed a hand over her head. "No. There are rumors that it was murder, but Donovan died of illness. He didn't want anyone to know he was sick, because they'd start making a ruckus about who would take over the shop. I like to think that your uncle was called up to the great cauldron above a little before his time."

"So what about the note that Ebenezer talked about? The one you said didn't exist?"

Betty tugged at her collar as if it was getting hot in here. She glanced over at the hearth and clapped her hands. "Soups on. Want some? It's an old family recipe. One you should've tried years ago, but as they say, better late than never."

My stomach rumbled. I'd only had nibbles at the party. A hearty meal sounded great, even if it was heavy for summer fair.

"Sure."

Betty rose. She snapped her fingers, and a bowl and plate appeared. She snapped them again, and a slice of cornbread disappeared from the skillet and plated itself. The duo floated over to me, and I paused before I took it, unsure of how much pressure to apply.

"Take it and my magic will vanish. It should give easily," she said as if reading my mind.

It was as she said. Thick, rich stock with full beef flavor revved my taste buds. The cornbread crumbled easily into the stew.

"Crisco sure did the trick."

Betty smiled. "You'd be surprised how handy it can come. Here."

She snapped her fingers again, and a tub appeared in front of me. "All kinds of help to witches. Keep it in your purse. That's where I keep mine."

She sat down with a heavy sigh. "About Donovan—someone got it in their head to start a story that a note had been found saying that the new owner of Familiar Place would be murdered too. I've never seen such a note. No one that I know has. It's only a rumor, nothing else."

"So, exactly what kind of illness took Donovan?"

"Your uncle liked his hard cider. One night he got into a bad batch and drank so much he gave himself a bout of poisoning that he couldn't recover from."

I frowned. "That doesn't sound like an illness."

She nodded. "We witches call it hard cider illness."

"I've never heard of it."

Grandma worked her bottom lip for a moment. "It's new."

Right.

"Anyway, Donovan wrote the letter to you on his deathbed and used magic to send it to you. But it's up to you to keep that shop open. It's important, not only to this town, but to the entire witching world. People come from all over to find their familiars. You'll see. I'll show you tomorrow."

I smiled feebly. "Sure. I can't wait to find out," I lied.

Okay, so there was a suspicious death and a roomful of rumors swirling around. Let's not sugarcoat things; even though Betty said Donovan's death was illness, there were still questions about what caused him to get sick—at least in my mind. And a note that existed but didn't exist. On top of that, I was the prime suspect in a murder, and all the crap was hitting the fan like crazy. I'll admit, I needed a way out of my other life, but this wasn't it.

The only thing was, I wasn't going to be in Magnolia Cove tomorrow to find out. Because I had a plan, and that plan meant breaking out of this town tonight.

SEVEN

Betty showed me to my room. "It was your mother's," she said, hiding a sniffle behind the wig she held in her hand.

I walked through, noting all the trophies for spell casting and pictures. I caught a glimpse of red hair in a frame. My breath hitched at the sight of the woman staring back at me.

She had been beautiful. Gold spooled in her long crimson hair, and her eyes were a deep blue. She didn't have one speck of the freckles constellating my face or the brown eyes I had.

I thanked Betty and for a moment, hesitated. Part of me wanted to reach out and hug her. She was, according to Mattie, my Me-Me.

I wanted to hug Betty, I really did, but a coil of pain from past hurts stopped me.

After she left, I sat on the bed. I fished my phone from my purse and dialed Caleb's number.

"Hey, babe, I thought you were going to call when you got off work?"

"Yeah," I said, "about that. Strange stuff has happened today. Let me tell you—"

But I couldn't tell him, could I? If I did, I'd lose my power.

Right.

What power? My schizophrenic ability to hear voices that appeared to come from animals?

"Yeah, babe, can I call you tomorrow? I've been busy with fantasy football. This is taking more of my time than I thought."

I frowned. "What does that mean?"

"I've been thinking…maybe we should focus on our own stuff right now, you know? Maybe not focus on each other so much."

A woman laughed in the background. "Who's that?"

"Oh, uh, just Jody's cousin, Amanda. So, what do you say?"

I laughed. It started as a bubble in the back of my throat, but by the time it caught air, it became a full-on maniacal sound, one filled with failure and insanity.

Which is exactly how I felt.

"Sure, Caleb. Let's call it quits. That's actually the most perfect ending to my day. I've been fired from my job, chased by a madman who thinks it's okay to stand on cars, and accused of murder. Sure. Let's break up. End it. Listen, do me a favor and have a great life on me."

I pressed the Off button and tossed the phone on the floor. I had lain on the bed for exactly two seconds when a knock sounded.

"Come in," I said, sounding about as deflated as a dead jellyfish on the beach looked.

Amelia and Cordelia tucked their heads in. Amelia fluffed her short hair. "Hey, we just wanted to say good night, and offer you some clothes so that you can get out of those."

I shrugged. "Sure. You got anything in black? 'Cause I'm in mourning for my life."

Amelia laughed. "Cuz, we're going to use magic to create a new look for you."

I almost perked up at that. Almost. The sound of using magic to create a wardrobe made me think my options were pretty much limitless.

"We can create whatever you want," Cordelia said. "And we can show you how, too."

I sat up. "Okay. I'm in. Can you also take ten pounds off my butt and put it in my boobs?"

Amelia laughed. "No, but you can if we teach you how to create a glamour. First things first. Want some pajamas?"

"Yes. Cotton please. Simple. No pattern."

Cordelia split from Amelia. "Color?"

"Black."

Cordelia clapped her hands together, and half a second later my clothes were gone, replaced by simple black pjs.

I jumped from the bed. "Holy crap. That's so super amazing." I ran my hands down the legs. Smooth as silk and the fit was perfect.

"Show me how to do that," I said. "Please. Please. Please."

"Okay," Amelia said, "the first thing you have to do is feel the magic within you. Do you feel it?"

I cringed. "I don't know. Where would I feel it?"

Cordelia plopped down on the only chair in the room, a floral recliner. She crossed one long leg over the other. "It's different for everyone. Sometimes it feels like a flutter in your stomach. Sometimes it feels like heartburn that you have to get rid of."

I frowned. "I don't have any feelings like that."

"Maybe it's behind your eyes," she said. "Like a migraine waiting to happen. Or a toe cramp. I once knew a witch who felt magic in her little toe and knew it was primed to use when her foot hurt."

I shook my head. "No. I don't have anything like that."

Cordelia glanced at Amelia. "We can still try to teach her, I guess."

Amelia took my hands. "I'm going to give you some of my magic, but since most of your power probably has to do with your ability to communicate with animals, I'm not exactly sure how this is going to work, yet we can try."

Just then the door opened and Mattie padded inside. She took a spot on the windowsill and started licking a paw and washing her face.

Amelia said, "Are you ready to work some magic?"

"This should be interesting," Mattie said.

My gaze flickered to her. The cat's whiskers twitched. I decided to ignore her barb.

Warm liquid energy flooded into me. It hummed and vibrated, thrumming through my body tight like a wound violin string. This was magic. I could feel it. It sparked in my chest and flowed like water through my veins.

I beamed at Amelia. "I feel it."

"Now try to use it."

"How?"

"Reach out with your mind. See it change into whatever you want."

So I tried. I tried to wrap my mind around it and mold it, but all I felt was a fizzle as the power drained from me.

Amelia smiled. "We'll try again tomorrow."

I sank back onto the bed. "So I didn't get it?"

Cordelia looked up from the cell phone she was scrolling through. "No."

I laughed bitterly. "I'm supposed to be a witch. Some great witch who can communicate with animals, but I can't work a lick of magic."

"It takes time," Amelia said encouragingly. "Not everyone does it right off. I did, and Cordelia did, but most people don't."

"That doesn't make me feel any better," I mumbled. Forcing a smile, I said, "Thanks, anyway. We can work more on it tomorrow, I guess."

Cordelia unlinked her legs and rose. "Come on. Let's give our new cousin some alone time. I know it's been a day."

"You don't even know the half of it," I said.

Amelia flashed two rows of teeth in a tight smile. "We heard about Ebenezer. Whole town has by now."

"First day here and I'm already making an awesome name for myself."

Amelia wrapped me in a swift hug. "Don't worry about it. Grandma will help you. She has a lot of clout in the community."

Did she call threatening to give a policeman purple mumps clout?

"Okay," I said, pushing forward a feeble smile. "Thanks."

"I've got your back," Amelia said. "If anyone mentions it at town hall, I'll shut them right on down."

I quirked a brow. "Town hall?"

She nodded. "That's where I work. Filing permits and such. Cordelia works at the inn."

Cordelia smiled. "Yep. I can tell you who's coming and going in Magnolia Cove."

"Thanks," I said. "I'll remember that." They said their good nights and left. I glanced at Mattie. "Are you sleeping in here?"

"I was your mom's cat."

At the mention of my mother liking the cat, I bristled. "I don't like cats."

Mattie blinked at me. "Probably best you learn 'cause you'll start to find that animals like you. A lot, sugar."

I slid under the covers and snapped off the light. "Good night."

As much as I didn't want to, I did fall asleep, but told myself I had to wake early. Super early. Like three a.m. early so that I could sneak out of town.

Yes, I know Todd the Policeman said they would come after me, but I didn't even have a place to live anymore. So I could at least sell the key at the nearest pawnshop and head west with a good chunk of money because I was pretty sure that key was made of gold.

Had I ever dodged anything in my life?

Yes, I'd bounced a few checks, but I'd never killed someone. By the time I was in Las Vegas or wherever, the police should've found the real killer.

I slipped from the covers, grabbed my purse and headed out the door. The vine didn't bother me as I padded across the porch and back to Bubbling Cauldron, where my car was parked.

I hitched the door open as quietly as possible and slid in. The temperamental piece of shinola rumbled to life, and I slinked down the road, heading out of Magnolia Cove forever.

I got about a minute outside the town when my car stalled. "Dang it! This piece of crap. First thing I'm doing with the money is buying a brand-new car that no one's even farted in."

I shoved open the door and popped the hood. What the heck could be wrong with the stupid thing now? Old age?

I sighed as a dark flash swept past me. I whirled around, heart in my mouth and fingers trembling.

"Who's there?"

No answer.

Then a rustle from the bushes and out stepped the man in black. You know, the one with the long hair who attacked me? The Rufus guy. The one who thought it was normal to stand on the roof of someone's car.

A blue flame flickered from his fingers. "Come with me," he said in a low grumble.

I jutted out one hip. I was scared but also so irritated with men that this guy was about to get all my anger.

"You know, I'm really tired of you men thinking you can just do whatever you want with me, that I don't have a say in things. Well, I do. And I don't know what you want, but I'm sure as heck not going anywhere with you and that ridiculous blue flame. What is that? Is it supposed to scare me or something?"

Rufus balked, glancing at his flame and then to me. He shook his head as if shaking my words off and said, "You will come with me!"

"Is that all you can say?"

The flame grew. Rufus drew back his hand as if he was winding up for a pitch, and released the orb of light right at me.

Something knocked me from my feet. A gush of air rushed from my lungs as I hit the ground hard. The world scrambled as the blue light whizzed past my head. Shards of earth blew into the air, exploding.

A dark shape appeared in front of me. It was a man. Another one. Great. Not that I'm a man-hater and angry at all men, but right now I wasn't exactly a fan, thanks to good ole Mr. Fantasy Football.

A green light emanated from the second figure. "Get out of here, Rufus. This isn't your territory."

The green light pitched forward, shooting straight at Rufus. In a blink the dark figure shrank into a vertical line and vanished.

I sat in silence for a moment, unsure of exactly what had happened. A hand appeared in front of my face, and I recognized Axel, aka Mr. Sexy.

I slid my fingers over his palm as his hand closed on mine. Warmth danced over my skin, sending a tingle sweeping up my arm.

"You okay?" he said.

He pulled me to my feet like I weighed nothing more than a sip of air. "Yes. Thank you."

The moon beamed across his face. His blue eyes appeared crystalline in the white glow. "You shouldn't be out here by yourself."

I brushed dirt from my rear. "Yeah, well, nobody's perfect. I didn't expect that guy to be out here."

Axel cocked a brow. "You didn't expect him to be waiting for you, you mean? Rufus is on your tail, so he's going to be waiting for you to leave so he can take you."

A chill crept down my arms. "Why? What does he want?"

Axel reached for me. "Come on, let's get you back into town."

I slipped from his grasp. "No. I want some answers. No one in this town just simply tells me the truth."

His lips curled into an amused smile. "The truth is that I was out here looking for clues in the death of Ebenezer Goldmiser. I saw you trying to leave town when you know you're a suspect in the case, and then Rufus shows up, apparently intent on stealing you for some reason. You're a brand-new witch with no idea how to use your power. I show up to help you, am able to send Rufus running for the hills and now you're standing in the middle of the forest, still completely exposed, yelling at me. You're welcome."

My mouth opened and shut like a fish gulping air. "Thank you," I said weakly.

He turned to walk back into the forest. "You're welcome."

I speed walked to catch up with him. "Listen, I'm sorry I was rude back there. It's just been a horrible day. You would think that discovering you're a witch is great and awesome, but I'm not crazy about animals and now they think I murdered this Ebenezer guy. I can barely butter a piece of toast with a knife, much less use one to slice and dice."

Axel grunted. "You want me to push your car off the road?"

I grimaced. "Yeah. Sure. Thanks."

He stopped, turned back around, and we pushed my Camry onto the shoulder. "I'll call someone about it in the morning," I said.

We headed down the road. "Didn't you say you were looking for clues to Ebenezer's death?"

Axel nodded. "The family hired me to do my own investigation."

I sneaked a glimpse of him in the moon's glow. Hard jaw, high cheekbones, piercing eyes—yep, there was a reason the women in the town referred to him as Mr. Sexy.

"Do they not trust the police—to hire you, I mean?"

He shrugged. "People often hire me. Just because."

Okay, whatever that meant.

"So what've you discovered so far about Ebenezer's death?"

His head slanted as he gazed at me. I flashed him a huge smile. The sort of smile people will tell you to tone down, keep it smaller because you look like you're trying too hard. Yep, I was trying too hard, and I wasn't ashamed to admit it.

"I haven't discovered anything because as soon as I started, I saw a flash of blue and Rufus trying to seize you."

"Wow, you must have some awesome eyesight."

He didn't say anything to that. "Can I walk you home?"

I shook my head. "No. I want to help you."

"I work alone."

I shrugged. "I'm on the line for this murder. You know how folks are in small Southern towns. You look like you're not from there, and they think you're a spy or something. They don't trust you, and they're ready to accuse you of a crime whether or not you did it."

Axel didn't say anything.

"I won't get in the way. Look, I'm not going to beg, plead and steal, here. You did me a favor—huge favor, maybe even saved my life—so if you don't want me to come, I won't, but I want to have some shape in my destiny. Since yesterday nothing has been in my control, and I'm tired of it."

He stopped, pivoted toward me. "You're not going to cry about it, are you?"

I sniffed, gauged my tear-making machine. "No, I don't think so—why?"

He placed his hands on his hips and shifted his weight. "Because I really hate it when women cry. It's just the worst."

Hope sparked deep in my chest. "You're saying if I start crying, you'll have to do what I want?"

Axel shook his head. "Nope. Definitely not."

I cocked my head. "I think you're lying."

"I do not lie."

"Not even a white lie? Everyone tells those now and again. You have to."

He waved his hands in front of his body. "I'm completely transparent."

I scoffed. "No one's that perfect."

"But anyway, I work alone. You can't come with me."

I hated to do it, I really did, but it was the only shot I had at putting my destiny in my own hands. Reaching deep down into my core, I found a hidden box where I'd stuffed all my angst and frustration at what I'd lost over the course of twenty-four hours.

It took about three seconds for that to ignite into full-blown tears. Really, it was easy—about the easiest tears I'd ever shed.

"What are you doing?" he said.

"I'm-I'm— It's all so—horrible."

His face pinched into a look of disbelief. "What are you doing?"

"I'm trying to-to— I know—you hate it when people cry—but it's —be-be-been so rough."

I pulled myself back from a wailing ugly cry, because I wanted to keep some of my dignity—at least what little I had left, but really there was no other choice.

"Will you stop crying? You'll wake up the entire town."

"Ca-ca-can I come wi-with you?"

He sighed, rolled his eyes and scraped the ground with his boot. "Yes. For heaven's sake stop that crying."

I sniffled a few times and brushed the tears from my cheeks. My head throbbed from congestion, but it would pass soon.

"Thank you," I said.

Axel shot me a look so scathing I almost shrank back. "Come on. But keep quiet and stay behind me."

"Okay," I said, giving myself an invisible fist bump of victory.

I silently followed Axel around to the back of Bubbling Cauldron Road to the row where Ebenezer's pawnshop and my pet store sat. Axel fished something from his pocket. Moonlight glinted off metal.

"You have a key?" I said, surprised.

He nodded. "Ebenezer's family gave it to me." Axel unlocked the door and pushed it open. I started to follow him in, but he grabbed hold of me.

A warm, electric current swam up my arm. My heart pinged as if someone plucked the organ. I glanced up into eyes that looked more silvery than blue in the night. Long, dark lashes filled my view as his gaze darted from my face off to the side.

He'd felt it, too.

The power running between us.

Well, whatever. I didn't have time for men. They were nothing but a handful of trouble and a watershed of tears.

Axel's hands dropped from my arms. He pointed to the ground. "Watch that."

He knelt and I followed. Tracking away from the back door were small footprints.

"What are those in?" I said.

"Blood," he said without looking up. "Cat paw prints. And they're fresh."

I cracked the knuckles on my right hand. "I didn't see a cat when I was in there."

"Well, there was one," he said, "and from the looks of it the animal stepped right through the blood around Ebenezer's body and came out here."

"How? Can it walk through walls?"

Axel shrugged. "Maybe."

"That's ridiculous. Animals don't walk through walls."

His lips pinned into a line. "You'd be surprised about things around here."

I brushed locks of hair from my eyes. "I guess that's true. But where do the prints go?"

Axel rose, studied the tracks. "Looks like they went someplace you're familiar with."

I rose, my knee catching as I straightened. I shook off the twinge of pain. "Where's that?"

He nodded down the street. "Right into your shop."

EIGHT

I backed up. "In there? In my shop? What if it's a feral cat waiting to kill me?"

Axel scrubbed a hand down his face. The sandpapery sound reminded me of normalcy in this otherwise abnormal town.

"Let me guess—you're not an animal person."

"I'm barely a people person," I said.

"I can tell."

I fisted a hand to my hip. "What's that supposed to mean? Like you don't even know me. You're not allowed to make sweeping generalizations about my behavior."

He chuckled. "It's not too hard when you're fleeing town in a broken-down car and barely even think to thank me for saving your life."

I scoffed. "I thanked you."

"Only because I lit a fire under your rear."

"No, you didn't... Wait. Listen, I don't need this drama in my life."

He flashed me a smile that made my stomach curl into a knot. A good knot, not a bad knot—not the kind where you know you've got to make it to the bathroom within four seconds. No, this was the kind that dug under my skin, pulsing to life on its own. The sort

SOUTHERN MAGIC

of reaction that started as a flutter and bloomed into a full-on tingle.

He shrugged, and a dimple winked from his right cheek. "You don't need to ask for trouble. Apparently it's seeking you out."

"I didn't do anything to get it."

"Ever heard of karma?"

I stopped cold in the alley. "Are you accusing me of being a terrible person who's called down a flood of drama into my life?"

He smiled. "No. I'm talking about Ebenezer. If anyone was asking to get murdered, it was that guy. Besides, are you going to make me beg you to let us into the store? It's the only way to see where the cat went."

"No," I scoffed. "I'm not going to make you bed—beg, I mean. *Beg.* Nowhere was I thinking about bed, or beds, or bedrooms or even darkened lampshades."

What was wrong with me?

He killed a smile that had etched out on his face. "No, it's fine. Seriously. Let's just get inside."

I snapped my trap shut and fished the key from my purse. Sighing, I shoved it into the back lock. "I've only tried this on the front door, so I don't know if it works back here."

"It'll work," he said.

The locked turned, and I pushed open the door. I flipped on a switch and found a dark hallway with a bathroom and what looked like a storage room and an office. From here I could see the front of the store.

My chest constricted as the animals stirred to life. Not wanting to look like a total crazy woman in front of Mr. Sexy, I avoided cupping my hands over my ears to stop the deluge of voices I was afraid were coming.

Instead I threw my shoulders back and stepped forward as if I owned the place—which I did—and managed to plunge my foot in a bowl of cold water.

"Ah." I tumbled forward, losing my balance and pitching toward the floor.

Solid arms grabbed me around the waist. I immediately sucked in, wanting to make my form as small and petite as possible even though I was completely average sized.

"There you go," he said, righting me.

I brushed invisible ego from my pants. "I haven't spent much time in here."

"I can tell," he said. "Your animals look dazed."

I glanced around at the pups and kittens as they yawned to life. "What'd you mean?"

He raked his fingers through his dark hair. It shone like he had really healthy tresses. It was the kind of thick, wavy hair a girl would gouge someone else's eye out for.

Wait. Was that too violent?

Sorry.

Axel leaned against the shiplap wall. "When your uncle owned the place, the animals would perk up as soon as he stepped in. They all loved him."

My head tipped toward the ceiling in defeat. "Yeah, well the difference between him and me is that I don't like animals."

He quirked a brow. "As you said."

"Yeah," I said, "they make me sneeze. I'm allergic."

He frowned. "Okay. Well, let's find this cat. Try not to scare it with your innate hatred of its being."

I shook my head. "What does that even mean? Why would I hate it?"

He raked his knuckles over his chin. Something told me that he was giving me a hard time. "You just said you don't like animals. I want this creature to think we like it. I don't know about you, but if I don't think someone likes me, I'm not going to like them back."

"What about loving your fellow man?"

He patted the air. "Hold on, partner. After I've tried and failed at loving my fellow man, then a hint of dislike might creep in. I don't go in not liking someone—unlike you and your dislike of animals."

Heat flushed my cheeks. "Why are you giving me such a hard time?"

SOUTHERN MAGIC

He shrugged. "Just pointing out the obvious."

"This is why you're not dating anyone, right? Because you needle them?"

Axel's jaw fell. "Excuse me. How did we get started on my love life? And you don't even know me."

A slow smile curled on my lips. I had him. "No, I don't know you any more than you know me, but that didn't stop you from pegging me up on a wall, locking me in a box and throwing away the key."

He rocked back on his heels. "Okay. Point taken. I'll cease and desist with all presumptuous thoughts."

"Thank you… Now, let's find the cat."

We followed the footprints to the office. Axel pushed open the door. Sitting on a chair was a small calico cat. The creature shivered as if a cold wind was continually blowing on it. It blinked green eyes at us and scrambled up the back of the seat.

"Shh," Axel said. "Calm down. No one's here to hurt you."

The cat stopped and stared at us. Axel elbowed me. "Time to talk to it."

My head whipped up a double take faster than you can say *shrimp and grits*. "Talk to it? What do you mean?"

"That's what you do, isn't it? Talk to animals? See what it knows about Ebenezer's death."

Outside the door, the animal squawking started up. I could hear them wondering what I was doing in the store and if I was going to feed them, 'cause boy they sure were hungry.

I shut the door to close out the noise. The cat leaped from the chair onto the desk.

"Calm down," Axel said. "No one wants to hurt you. We're sorry about what happened to Ebenezer."

The cat's head rattled atop its neck. The creature was clearly scared and obviously alone if it was coming down to my shop for safety. It must not've heard there was a new owner in town—an animal-disliking owner.

Axel stepped forward. "We're here to help."

The creature's eyes widened in terror. It skidded across the table, sending paperwork flying in every direction. It shot to the floor and under the desk.

"I don't think it likes you, either," I said.

"I didn't claim to be a cat whisperer," he said.

"Good thing," I muttered. I rounded the desk and bent down.

The cat had wedged itself way in back. "Food. Let's get it some."

Axel hooked his fingers on his belt loops, swaying his hips in a way that made my flesh tingle. "Great idea. Know where he keeps the chow around here?"

"No clue. But you stay here and I'll find it."

I found the kibble easily enough in the storage room in a big bin. I shoveled out a handful and dropped it in a bowl I found nearby. By the time I returned to the room, Axel was sitting cross-legged in the back of the desk, sweet-talking the animal.

"It's okay," he cooed. "No one's going to hurt you."

"You're blocking its only path of escape."

Axel glanced up as I came around. "I'm trying to coax it out."

"More like scare it to death," I muttered. "Here's the food."

I handed him the bowl. He set it down and backed up. "How about I give the expert a try?"

"Great. Where's the expert?" I said. I waited for Axel to answer, but all he did was stare at me. "Oh, you mean me. Right. Expert. Okay. Let me do my thing."

I hooked my head over the desk. The cat was staring at the food. I sat down, being sure to give the creature enough room to scatter if it needed to.

I cleared my throat. "Ahem. Okay. Hi. I've never done this before. My name's, um, Pepper and sometimes I can hear things."

"That makes you sound crazy," Axel murmured.

"Well, maybe I am for believing I'm in a town full of witches and hanging out in a store in the middle of the night with a private detective everyone in town calls Mr. Sexy."

"What?" he said.

"Never mind," I said quickly. I turned back to the cat. "If you want to talk to me, you can. I can help you. Both of us will. We're sorry about what happened to Ebenezer, but we can help if you tell us what you saw."

The cat stared at me for a moment, and then it leaned forward tentatively, sniffing. I held out my palm and it took a good whiff and a small pink tongue flickered over its mouth. A moment later it was nudging my hand, and against my better judgment, I found myself stroking the animal between its ears.

After a few minutes the cat curled into my lap, settling with several large claws kneading into my legs before forming a tight ball and purring itself to sleep.

"I guess that's a start," I said.

Axel glanced over and chuckled. "I'll take it. Is she asleep?"

"I think so. And what makes you call it a 'she'?"

He leaned one hand on the desk. "It's a calico. They're female."

I blinked down at the tiny frail creature. "Oh. I didn't know that."

"There's probably a lot you don't know about animals."

I rolled my eyes. "That obvious, huh?"

He pinched two fingers together. "Slightly."

"Great."

"Listen, why don't you put her down? We'll leave her in here, grab some breakfast and come back, see if she's ready to talk."

I frowned. "First of all, this is an animal who can walk through walls. She might not be here when we return. Secondly, how do you know she can talk? And what if she's not even Ebenezer's cat?"

Axel pulled a phone from his back pocket. "I'm going to check on the pet cat situation with Ebenezer's kids, and you're right about the walking thing. I'm going to find a cat carrier in this place, and we'll bring her with us. If she tries to walk through the carrier, at least we'll be there."

I scoffed. He was a tad cocky to think I was just going to jump when he said to. "What makes you think I'm hungry?"

He shrugged. "Just figured. Getting chased by Rufus, helping me talk to animals, thought you might be. I worked up an appetite from it. I thought you might've, too. Besides, I'm buying."

"What's open at four a.m.?"

"The Spellin' Skillet. Great little place on the other side of town." He slid a hand down his flat stomach. "Anyway, I thought it would give us a chance to talk. There's a lot I can help you with when it comes to this store. Let me grab a carrier."

I waited patiently for him to return. He shuffled behind the desk and set the carrier down. I gently put the cat inside. She opened one eye but then snuggled back into sleep when I zipped the door shut.

I brushed my hands and pushed off the floor. The amount of gentleness that Axel used as he tucked the cat under one arm surprised me.

I opened the office door. "So exactly how can you help me out when it comes to this store?" I led us back out the door, promising myself that I'd come back after breakfast and at least check that the water dishes were full and feed the rest of the animals, even though it appeared they slept when I wasn't there.

Axel flashed me a smiled as I locked up. "I can help you because besides your uncle, I know the most about Familiar Place."

"How's that?" I said, flipping the lock.

Axel's eyes darkened. "Because I used to come every day. Your uncle trusted me with his secrets, Pepper. He trusted me with his life."

NINE

The Spellin' Skillet was like a country general store for witches. Oh, and it had a restaurant tucked in back behind magical cast-iron skillets molded into frogs and bats instead of corn husks.

Yep. This was quite a culture shock.

A hostess wearing a black dress that looked to be made of cobwebs and leather instead of cotton and polyester, greeted us.

"Your usual table, Mr. Reign?"

Axel nodded. He kept his head tipped down as she led us to the back, way back of the restaurant, to an area blocked off from the rest of the dining room. I glanced around nervously, waiting for a small man stroking a cat to show up and demand money or else he'd break my thumbs.

Just kidding. I figured the mafia wasn't going to be in the Spellin' Skillet.

Well, let's just say I hoped not.

I settled into a booth across from Axel. "You must be pretty special around here."

He shrugged. "Not special. I just like my privacy."

I glanced around. "This looks pretty private. About as private as you can get unless you're on the moon."

He pulled a band from his pocket and wrapped his hair into it, securing it at the nape of his neck. I had to say, with the hair swept from his face, Mr. Sexy was even more handsome than he was with all that hair down.

Just sayin'.

"Do you want the cat on your side?" he said.

"Oh, yeah. I don't know. I mean, this is kind of your area. You found her."

He pushed up his sleeves. "But she was in your store, so that makes her more yours than mine."

I grimaced. "Sure. I'll take her."

He handed me the carrier, and I tucked it in beside me. I glanced at the menu. "What's good here?"

Axel popped open his own menu. "The omelets are great. There's also witchin' skillets—those are hash browns, eggs, sausage, cheese all cooked together in a little skillet."

"Too bad there aren't any jelly beans in it."

He quirked a dark brow. I shrugged. "I love jelly beans. Sue me. But anyway, I'm sold on the skillet. With a cup of strong coffee to wash it all down. I get the feeling I'm going to be exhausted later on."

The waitress returned, and we ordered. When she left, I settled back into the booth. "So, there are so many things I want to ask you."

The waitress returned with coffee, and Axel sipped his. "Like what?"

"Well, I'm going to ignore the mafia environment of the private room and skip straight to the part about my uncle. What do you mean that he trusted you with his secrets and his life?"

Axel smiled. "First question I would ask. Smart. I knew your uncle a long time. Let's just say, he understood certain aspects about me, about my family."

I pressed my lips together to the point that they buckled past a pout. "But you're a witch?"

"A wizard, technically, with other abilities. I'm a private investigator, as you know. Donovan often hired me to watch out for him. Guard him, that's what I meant by he trusted me with his life. We were close. He was a good man, and he thought very highly of you."

I glanced behind me to make sure Axel was talking to me. "What? I didn't even know him. How could he speak highly of me?"

He tapped a cup of cream on the table and tore off the paper top. "He kept tabs on you. Your whole family has."

"Even that crazy Betty?"

He threw his head back so far his Adam's apple bobbed when he laughed. "Yes. Even her. She's something else. Do you know one time she spelled this entire town to sleep so that she could streak through it naked?"

"What? Why?"

He rested his elbows on the table. "Because she could, basically. Wanted to do some ritual by herself and didn't want anyone to see that body of hers, so she put the whole town into a deep sleep."

My interest piqued at my jean-jumpsuit-wearing grandmother. "Wow. That's impressive."

"Your uncle expected your animal talents to be impressive as well."

"How so?" I gestured stop. "What I mean is, I can hear them, but how is that helpful or important?"

Axel dipped his head toward the carrier. "Get her to talk and we may know who killed Ebenezer. But more than that, you help witches find familiars."

I waved my hand, fatigued from all the drama associated with my so-called ability. "Whatever that means. Listen, all I hear when I go in that shop is a jumble of whining, annoying creatures."

"That's because you haven't spent time with them. I can help you."

I'm pretty sure my eyes sparkled with something—delight? Gratitude? A lifeline in the ocean of witchery that I was a newbie in?

Yeah. Probably the last one.

"What about Rufus? What does he want with me?"

Axel wrapped his knuckles on top of the table. "That's a very interesting question. No telling. Maybe he wants you to talk to an ostrich for him, figure out what it needs. Maybe he wants to drain your power. Rufus is no good."

I frowned. "That's an understatement. He told me I'd die if I didn't go with him. So it's either go with him or die for not? Sounds dangerous."

Axel sighed. "He's had some run-ins with the law but manages to get out of any trouble because his family's rich. Though he can't come into Magnolia Cove; the community doesn't trust him. One time he tried to play vampire on a local girl."

"Vampire?"

Axel nodded. "Yeah. He's a warlock not a vampire. Almost killed her. That's when we stopped letting him into town."

The waitress appeared with our plates. My skillet of cracked golden eggs, sausage, cheese and hash browns was like the best thing I had ever seen in my entire life. I squirted a dollop of ketchup on top and chowed down.

"Oh wow," I said between moans. "This is amazing."

"You're welcome," Axel replied.

I hid my laugh behind a napkin. "Thanks for bringing me here, but seriously—why are you all the way in back?"

He sighed. Oh, this was going to be good.

"I have…let's just say certain abilities that people find disconcerting. They don't like it. So to keep the population at rest and give myself privacy, I sit back here."

I shook my head. "I don't understand. From the way the women talked, you were the most eligible bachelor in town."

His blue eyes sparked. Crap. I probably shouldn't have told him.

"They think I'm the most eligible bachelor in town. No one's ever told me that."

I shrugged. "Well, unless you have your own TV show advertising it, you probably wouldn't know."

He frowned. "I'm not interested in that. I'm interested in figuring out who killed Ebenezer, and helping you with the store."

I jabbed a hash brown with my fork. "Why do you want to help me with the store?"

He paused. "Your powers are unique and special. They can help a lot of folks."

I sighed. "Yeah. Great. I'm not an animal lover. People who own pet stores should love animals. I don't. Now, give me a jewelry store. That would've been awesome. I could run that easily."

Axel chuckled. "Give me a car garage, same thing. But sometimes, you never know what good things can come out of something. You just have to stay positive and open-minded."

"I'll try to remember that."

Axel nodded. "Okay. So when we finish breakfast, how about I show you a little bit about your store? About how to communicate and help someone find their familiar?"

I cringed. "Er. Um. Sure."

"It's nothing to be scared about, I promise."

Maybe he could tell my knotted stomach that, because I wasn't feeling so confident.

But anyway, we finished up breakfast, which Axel paid for. I knew y'all would be asking. Seemed he was a good Southern boy who knew how to take a lady out to breakfast. We walked back to the shop as the sun was rising, sending long fingers like shadows jutting across the ground.

Once inside Familiar Place, I settled the cat on the counter. She still slept, by the way. Good. I could only handle one stressful situation at a time. I shrugged off my purse and for the first time realized I was wearing pajamas.

I glanced down at my clothes and back at Axel. "I think I'm going to have to go back to Betty's house before we open so I can change."

He shrugged. "It might be a good idea."

"Yeah, after this lesson, I'll do that." I clapped my hands. "Okay. Show me what to do."

He nodded. "Okay, so what's going to happen is that a witch will come into your store looking for a familiar." He splayed his hands. "Your uncle carried everything—any animal a witch could hope for. He always said the secret was listening to the creatures. Listen to the animals, they will tell you who they want. It's not the witch who chooses."

"But the creature," I said. I tapped a finger to my cheek. "But he's got toads and frogs, too. Do witches ever come here with bad intentions? I mean, I don't know anything about potions and spells, but I know about the stereotypical use of frog's eyes and bat wing."

Axel crossed his arms and smiled. "You have to watch for that. You'll be able to tell if someone has good intentions, and if you can't, just listen to the creatures, they'll let you know."

"We sure will," chimed a parrot.

"Thank you," I said.

"You're welcome," it squawked.

Axel rubbed his hands together. "Okay, so I walk in and say I need a familiar."

I stared at him. "Yeah. I don't know what to do."

He smiled, showing a flash of teeth. I was pretty sure one of them sparkled like diamonds, like you see in commercials when someone has a perfectly white smile.

He strolled the room. "The first thing your uncle would ask would be what sort of creature."

A lightbulb exploded in my brain. "Okay, right. What sort of animal do you like?"

Axel pretended to take in the room. "You know, I don't know. I like cats and I like dogs."

"Well, you have to pick one," I said, getting annoyed.

He wagged a finger at me. "Wrong answer."

"Too impatient?" I said.

He pinched his fingers together. "Slightly. You have to remember, when a witch picks a familiar, this is an animal they keep until one of them dies. It's a special relationship that you're helping to forge."

I tried not to roll my eyes. "Great. All right, you think you may want either a dog or a cat. Let me show you the puppies first."

"Good," he murmured.

Heat flared up my throat as Axel studied me. I felt like I was taking a test that foretold the rest of my life. No pressure.

I walked to the puppy bin and listened to them.

"Oh, I like him."

"He'd be a good master."

"Will he play with me every day?"

I tried to listen to every individual voice, but I had to admit it was hard to discern one from another.

"Your uncle also used to say when a person found their familiar, a sparkle occurred."

I cocked an eyebrow. "A sparkle?"

"Yes. Everything you're doing is right. All of it. He would lead the witch to animals and watch the interaction. When the sparkle happened, that was the match." Axel crossed back to the cat carrier. "Since I'm not really looking for a familiar, the sparkle won't happen, but it does happen when the right pair are put together."

"Okay, well that helps…" I guess.

He smiled. "Your business hours are posted on the door. You open at ten a.m. on Mondays."

"Well, at least that gives me time to shower and wrangle up some clothes," I said.

Axel nodded. "If you need help with the paperwork and stuff, Betty may offer suggestions for that. She ran a successful business in town for years."

I quirked a brow. "Really? What sort of business?"

"She ran the herb and potion store. She's a witch chemist by trade."

I frowned. "I thought she was a kitchen witch."

"That's the sort of witchcraft she can do. But her job was as the witch chemist."

"Really?"

He nodded. "Yeah. Don't let her fool you; she can heal you as easily as poison you."

I shrank back. "Wow. That does not make me feel confident about my grandmother."

He chuckled. "She's harmless. Mostly."

Axel grabbed the door handle and opened it. He paused, stared down the street.

"What is it?"

He glanced back at me. "Looks like someone's going into Ebenezer's store."

I crossed to him quickly, and sure enough, a woman wearing dark sunglasses and a handkerchief tied over her head had a key in the door and was unlocking it.

"Who's that?" I said.

Axel shook his head. "I don't know. But I'm about to find out."

TEN

I snatched my purse. "I'm coming with you."

Axel frowned. "No, you're not."

"Yes, I am."

He stared at me for a good long minute. I'm guessing he hoped his stare of death would make me change my mind. Ha-ha. Little did he know but I'm as stubborn as a bead of sweat rolling down the middle of your back on a blazing hot day. You know, the kind of day where you can't get cool and as soon as you walk out the door, your skin is on fire?

Yeah, that kind of stubborn bead of sweat—the kind that just don't stop popping up on your flesh under conditions such as those.

I jutted out one pajama-strapped hip. "Look, I'm on the hook for this murder. I'm coming with you, whether you like it or not."

Axel's gaze flickered to the shop.

"You better hurry. She might get away."

He threw me a scathing look and shot out the door. I followed him quick as mercury down the street and into the pawnshop.

There stood a short woman in a mink stole, large round red-framed glasses and so much gold it looked like she wore the inside of

Fort Knox. She hunched over the taped outline where Ebenezer's body had been.

I stopped short of Axel.

The woman didn't glance up at us, but she pulled a tissue from her purse and dabbed her cheeks. "It's true then, isn't it? My Ebie is gone."

Ebie? Hey, I guess even the strangest of folks can have a nickname.

"I'm sorry," Axel said.

"It's all right," she said. "I was out of town, honey, and I heard about what happened. I rushed right on over. It's terrible."

She blew her nose and glanced at us finally. "I'm Gilda Goldenheart."

"Axel Reign."

"Honey," she said softly, "you're the one they hired to help find out who did this, aren't you?"

"Yes, ma'am, I am."

Her gaze flicked to me in my pajamas, purse and shoes. A whirl of butterflies pumped through my stomach at how stupid I looked. "I'm Pepper Dunn."

"Oh, honey, are you the new person who's taken over the familiar shop?"

I nodded. "That's right."

"Such a shame about your uncle. It's like something's killing off everyone on the street." She grabbed her face. "It's horrible."

Her eyes rolled around the store. "Well, I just wanted to see what had happened to my Ebie. I see now it's true that he's gone."

I cleared my throat and stepped around Axel. Heck, I needed this lady to help me—she might offer clues as to who actually murdered Ebie.

"Ms. Goldenheart, were you and Ebenezer involved romantically?"

She clutched her heart. "Why, yes, honey. We were. We were hoping to get married this summer, but that's not going to happen now, is it?"

"I'm so sorry," I said. "And you were out of town, you say?"

"Oh yes, dear, I was down in Birmingham visiting some friends. I came back just as soon as I heard."

Axel swung to her other side and took Gilda's arm. "Would you happen to have their names and numbers?"

Gilda riffled through her purse. "Well, sure. Of course I'll get it to you, but right now I've got to get moving."

"Why's that?" I said.

"Well, honey, the lawyer's reading the will here in a few minutes."

"The will?" I said.

She nodded. "He's supposed to be. We're doing it over at Ebie's house. I know it's early for it to be read, but those were Ebie's instructions. He wanted the will announced as quickly as possible."

Axel nodded. "Good to know."

Gilda tightened the stole around her neck. "It was nice meeting both of you, but I need to get going."

Axel gestured for her to lead the way. "Of course."

We followed her out and watched as Gilda locked the shop and shuffled to her car.

I shot Axel a look. "Are you thinking what I'm thinking?"

Axel shook his head. "If you're thinking I'm going to the will reading and you're going to change clothes for your first day at the familiar shop, that would be about right."

I pressed a finger to the side of my mouth and pouted out my lips. "Um, I'm pretty sure you're going to take me because if you don't, I'm going to hand the mute kitten right back to you and you can see how much information you get out of it."

He shook his head. "You know that cat might tell you exactly who killed Ebenezer?"

I nodded. "I know, and I'm the only person who can hear it, if it decides to talk."

Axel rolled his eyes. "If you hand it to me, then you won't be able to get yourself off the hook."

I fisted my hands. "Okay, how about when the kitten does start talking, I go to the police instead of you? How're Ebenezer's kids paying you anyway? Only if you figure out the case? Or do you get a bonus if you crack it? The cat can help you crack it. *I* can help you crack it."

Axel sighed. "Okay. But let's get you a quick change of clothes and big sunglasses so no one recognizes you."

I laughed as I followed him to a '69 Mustang. At least, it looked like a '69. Heck in high heels, it might've been a '70. I don't know nothing about no cars, only that they're new or old, and this one was old.

I slid onto the buttery leather and said, "I don't think you should be worried about anyone in town recognizing me," I said, nodding toward a group of women strolling into the town coffee shop, Gargoyle's Grind.

"Why's that?" he said.

I smirked. "Because half the women in town have red hair. I'm as normal as can be around here."

WE REACHED BETTY'S HOUSE, which I'm guessing was now my house, about ten seconds later. Yes, y'all, that's how small this town is. Axel wanted to wait in the car, but afraid he'd ditch me, I yanked him inside.

Which is where I found Betty, sitting in a rocking chair facing the door, a shotgun over her knees.

"Whoa," I said, rearing back. "What are you expecting to come in that door?"

Betty put the shotgun down, lit a pipe and started puffing. Wow. I didn't know my grandmother smoked a corncob pipe. What else would I find out about her? Probably more than I wanted to know, like her streaking through Magnolia Cove.

"I was expecting whoever kidnapped you to come through, but I see you went with this man willingly." She hooked a fish eye on me. "Listen here, girlie. You're welcome to stay here, but I won't have one of my granddaughters running wild around this town with any Tom, Dick and Harry who she pleases. You may not've had any morals up in that Nashville place, but around here, we are A-list when it comes to morals. I've got morals up to my eyeballs."

I crossed my arms. "First of all, this isn't what you think. I have plenty of morals and do not go around throwing myself at men. Secondly, I heard you streaked through town and put everyone asleep so you could do so."

Betty pulled the pipe from her mouth. "Now how the heck would anyone know I did it if they were all asleep?"

I glanced back at Axel for help. "I mean, she's right. How do you know that?"

"Because she bragged about it later. Mrs. Craple, this is not what it looks like. I ran into your granddaughter trying to sneak out of town. Rufus was about to attack her, and I saved her from him and brought her back into town."

"Likely story," Betty said. "From now on, you're under curfew. You've got to be back in your bedroom at ten p.m. sharp."

I balked. I hadn't had a curfew in forever. But from the nasty snarl Betty had on her face, I did not want to tangle with her.

"Okay," I said. "I'll be in my bedroom every night by ten p.m. No problem. But now I need a change of clothes. We've got to run. We're trying to figure out who killed Ebenezer."

Betty nodded. "Fine. I'll be at the shop at ten to help you open. You may need me." She tapped her temple. "I have special talents."

"Great," I said.

"And you've got a full wardrobe in your closet now. Don't worry. I picked out every outfit by myself."

"Awesome," I said, dashing up the stairs to my mom's old bedroom.

Mattie stretched when I entered. "Someone made nice-nice with Mr. Sexy."

"No time to talk," I said. "I've got to jet."

I took a two-minute shower and riffled through the closet. Which held a variety of clothes from the seventies and eighties.

Oh crap.

My choices were either a polyester bodysuit with a paisley print and bell bottoms or a silver Michael Jackson jacket with shoulder pads that jutted out a mile in each direction.

Bodysuit it was.

I put on the bodysuit and was hoping Betty had at least left me some kind of curly-haired wig to complete the getup, but no dice.

So I towel dried my hair and put it into a messy bun. I found Axel downstairs and Betty with the shotgun draped over her legs again.

"Ready?" he said.

I nodded. "See you at the store," I said to Betty. "I don't think you'll need that shotgun."

"You never know," she said, eyeing Axel. "I might just bring it with me."

We hopped into the car and took a winding road out of town and up a hill to a tall gothic home. Stone gargoyles marked each side of the gate, and the tall windows and black shutters were more reminiscent of the Addams family than a pawnbroker.

And boy, were there a slew of cars in the driveway. Plenty of folks were heading inside. The women wore black dresses and the men wore black suits.

I eyed Axel's black ribbed shirt and jeans. "I guess we stick out like a sore thumb."

He slid into an empty spot and flipped off the starter. "Speak for yourself."

I threaded my fingers through a strand of wet hair. "It was between this and a Jackson Five reunion."

Axel grimaced. "I guess you made the right choice, then. Come on. They're probably about to start."

We slinked inside. A grand foyer greeted us. Dark wood floors, tall wainscoting and crystal chandeliers gave the home a rich, elegant look. Ebenezer had been such a miser, I figured he probably had a safe underneath the house stocked full of gold.

There was probably a leprechaun in it, too, guarding it.

Rows of seats were lined neatly facing the staircase. Axel pulled me off to the side. We stood behind a full-sized suit of armor. I could feel heat from Axel's body through my polyester pantsuit. His fingers tightened around my arm as he nodded toward the front.

There sat Gilda, stroking her mink stole.

Axel leaned over and whispered in my ear. "Some of the family who hired me are here, too."

"Which ones?"

He tipped his chin down toward me. His blue eyes swam in front of me. They were like liquefied sky. I felt a buzzing in my head and looked away.

He nodded discreetly at a long-legged blonde and a copper-headed man. "They hired me. Those are his kids."

I frowned. "But his nephew is a cop."

Just then, Todd the Policeman walked past us. I wedged myself farther behind the armor, hoping to stay as hidden as a woman wearing wallpaper could.

"The kids wanted an independent investigation—just in case."

"Just in case of what?"

A man moved to a lectern placed in the center of the room. He wore wire-rimmed glasses and a gray silk suit. His beard was neatly trimmed, and basically he had the tailored look of wealth dripping from him.

"Thank you everyone for coming," he said. "We're here to read the last will and testament of Ebenezer Goldmiser." He placed a slender box in front of him and retrieved a key from his pocket. He unlocked the box and opened the lid.

The lawyer stopped. Opened and shut the lid again. He glanced up and gazed at us. "Ladies and gentlemen, I'm not sure how to say this, but the last will and testament of Ebenezer Goldmiser is gone. It's been stolen."

ELEVEN

"Do you think the lawyer took it?" I said to Axel when we slipped back into his car.

Axel shook his head. "No, I don't believe so."

"Then who did? And how did they get access to it?" I said.

He flipped the ignition. "I don't know. I need some face time with the lawyer for that one."

"And so what happens now?" I said. "Who gets what?"

Axel grunted. "If the attorney has a copy of the will in his office, that's what he'll use."

I pushed my glasses onto my head. "What if it isn't the right copy?"

Axel shrugged. "How would anyone really know? Ebenezer might not've told his lawyer of any changes he made."

I frowned. "So theoretically someone would know about the changes, and maybe they didn't like said changes and stole the will?"

Axel shot me a charged look. "Or, we can jump ahead three paces before we know more about what's going on."

I shrugged. "It was just a theory."

"Ebenezer might've taken his will back to make adjustments. It could be in the house somewhere."

I folded my hands over one knee. "How're you planning to find out?"

He smiled. "I'm going to talk to the lawyer."

"Sounds great. When do we go?"

Axel chuckled. "There is no 'we' in this. You have to go to work, remember? Match people with their familiars and make all their magical dreams come true."

I rolled my eyes. "Yeah, right. And I'll do you another favor and see if I can get the cat to talk. Remember the cat? The one who might've been witness to a murder?"

"I remember. But the cat's not talking, and until she does, I've got other leads to follow up on."

Axel pulled into a spot in front of Familiar Place. It was nine thirty, which gave me a little time to get ready before we opened.

Get ready for what, I didn't know, but I could figure something out.

Axel told me he'd check on the cat later, so I got out and unlocked the door. First thing I did when I got in was refill all the waters, even though they were filled to the brim as it was, and gave all the animals their own scoops of food.

"We get two scoops," one of the puppies said.

"No, three scoops," another corrected.

I glanced down at the little white-and-black pups covered in silky fur. "Are y'all fibbing?"

"No, we don't know what fibbing is," said the first one.

I wagged my finger. "I'll give you one more scoop. But y'all have to promise not to eat so much that you get sick."

The puppies rolled happily over one another. "We promise!"

I gave them one more scoop of food and turned to the cat in the carrier. She was awake, and blinking those green eyes steadily at me.

"How about we get you out of there and let you roam awhile? Sound good? Only, you have to promise not to leave."

The calico simply stared.

"She doesn't want to talk," said one of the kittens. "But we talk."

"Thank you for clearing that up," I said.

I unzipped the carrier. The cat padded out slowly until she sat on the counter. She hunched down into a ball and coiled her tail around. She closed her eyes and purred.

Feeling sorry for her—she had just lost her owner—I scratched behind her ears, trying to get her to trust me enough to talk.

The door opened and in walked my newly acquired Grandma Betty. Today she was wearing white cowboy boots, jeans and a western-looking shirt with fringe on the back and front.

Was she going to a costume party? Looking down at my jumpsuit, I decided that perhaps she simply liked clothing that had a strong theme—Western wear for her, disco party for me.

"Good morning," I said.

She pointed a finger at me. "I'm watching you, kid. I don't know what living in the city did to you, but I'm watching and waiting."

I narrowed my eyes. "Waiting? For what?"

She puffed out her chest. "For you to make sure you're doing what you're supposed to be doing."

"I'm doing what I'm supposed to be. Heck, I'm not crazy about animals, but here I am, aren't I? I mean, it's not like I can leave this town. If I do, I'll either be arrested for a murder I didn't commit or carted off by some weird rock-star guy with blue flaming magic."

Betty pinched her lips. "Well, as long as we understand each other."

"We understand each other."

I didn't understand her at all.

The door opened again, and in walked a tall brunette with wide blue eyes. She wore a short skirt up to her neck, high heels and was being pulled by what looked to be a very eager ten-year-old.

"Aunt Idie Claire, they're all here. Every one of them! Just like you said."

My gut twisted so hard I might as well have wrung it out and pinned it to the clothesline outside. Holy jeez. This was my first customer. I could tell. An actual first customer. My fingers trembled as Betty shoved me toward them.

"I'm going," I muttered.

Betty tugged the fringe on her shirt. "Just making sure. You've got a legacy to live up to."

"Thanks," I said, walking off. I reached the little girl and her aunt. "Good morning, how're y'all doing today?"

The woman named Idie Claire—hold on, was that a joke?

"Is your name Idie Claire?" I said.

The woman smiled. "My grandmother always went around saying, 'I declare!' My mom thought 'I declare' was a person until she was a teenager. She thought it was so funny, she named me that."

Idie Claire glanced around the shop. "I declare!" She winked at me. "Y'all've got more animals than the zoo in the middle of a blizzard!"

Excuse me? "Yes, we've lots of animals," I said.

Her gaze slid over me. "You must be that new girl in town everyone's talkin' about. Nice to meet you. I'm Idie Claire Hawker. I do hair over at Spells and Shears. Listen, you ever want a haircut, you call me. And if you want to know anything else about town, you call me, too."

She slid me a card with a phone number on it. My gaze flickered over to Betty.

Idie Claire saw her and waved. "Well, hey, Betty Craple. You keeping all your clothes on today?"

Betty frowned. "As many as you got, Idie."

"Hope so." The hairdresser leaned over. "Bless your heart that she's your grandmother. There ain't no one like Betty Craple. God broke more than the mold when he made her. I'm pretty sure he burned it up in a fire right afterward. Maybe threw acid on it, too."

I stifled a laugh.

"I can hear you," Betty said. "I've got ears like a hawk has eyes. I use my magic to spy on people."

Idie Claire waved again. "You just keep right on listening. There's nothing I'm gonna tell her that I wouldn't say to you."

She smiled. "Anyhoo, I've brought my niece here to pick out her very first familiar. I'm guessing you can help us."

At this point I had two choices, look like I had no idea what I was doing and get a reputation for that—I mean, this was a small town and folks talk fast when something ain't right. Or I could fake it until I made it.

Yep. Much better choice.

I turned to the little girl. "What's your name?"

"Emily." She had the same bright eyes as her aunt.

"Emily, take my hand and we'll walk along the animals until you see one that you like."

Emily slid her hand into mine. I let her lead the way, twisting through the maze of rows that was the pet shop. She stopped at the puppies. They jumped and squabbled toward her. Emily stroked their heads and smiled, but I remembered that Axel said there would be a spark.

There wasn't one yet.

Then she wandered toward the birds. An African gray parrot settled its stare on her.

"She looks nice," it said in my head.

I turned to Emily. "Would you like to touch it?"

Emily shot me a secretive grin. "I don't know. He's got a big beak."

I laughed. "Well, we can just move right along, then."

We tromped over to the cage of kittens. Emily glowed when she saw them. Clearly cats were a favorite of hers.

"Let me play with her," one said in my head. It clawed up the cage, showing off its talents.

"No. Me." One from the back pushed its way to the front.

Emily slid her finger into the cage and stroked a couple. Still no spark.

"They're all so sweet," she said.

I had an idea. "Emily, why don't you tell me about your magic?"

She beamed. "Oh, my whole family has magic. All of them. Mine came in about a year ago, and it's grown so much. See?"

After releasing my hand, Emily took a step back. A light bloomed from her fingers. It floated up, a small bubble of an aura. Then it zoomed around the room, bouncing off walls and counters, zipping and snapping, weightless in its flight until it zoomed into Emily's mouth. She filled with light. She literally glowed.

It was so freaking cool.

As quickly as it started, her light vanished.

I clapped. "That was awesome."

"I have light magic," she said proudly.

"Well, that is super cool."

All that whizzing around gave me an idea. I took Emily's hand and said, "Come on."

In the very back of the bird display sat a pair of gorgeous rainbow-colored birds.

"We're rainbow lorikeet parrots," one snipped. "Not just birds."

Crap. Guess I'd better keep some thoughts to myself.

The other one cocked an eye at me. "And we go in pairs."

"Okay," I murmured. I turned to Emily. "What do you think of these? They go in pairs."

Emily's eyes widened. "They're beautiful."

I placed my hand down, hoping the bird would take the hint and jump on. It did. It fluttered up to my finger, and I held it out for Emily.

She smiled brightly as the bird waddled to her finger.

Then it happened.

The glow.

I was pretty sure I was the only person who could see it. Not sure how I knew that, but I did. Emily simply glowed from the inside the same way she had when her light zoomed into her body.

I picked up the other bird, and Emily extended the opposite hand for it.

The aura of light flushed from her again.

I smiled. So did Emily.

"So is that it?" I said.

Emily nodded. "I think so." She turned back to her aunt. "This is it, Aunt Idie. I've got two familiars."

The birds squawked and jabbered at me. I raised a hand to hush them. "They want you to use them with your magic," I told her.

Emily closed her eyes. The birds fluttered up and around her head. They created a formation, leaving a trail of magic in their wake. They fluttered back to Emily, landing on her shoulders, but they left a clear magical marker in the store from their flight path.

A heart made of light blazed where they'd flown.

Betty clapped. "Bravo, kid. You just used a familiar for magic. Great job."

Idie Claire paid for the birds while Emily played with her new familiars. The hairdresser cocked an eye at me. "You know, I just heard about that whole awful business with Ebenezer."

"Already?" I said, jaw dropping. "It just happened yesterday."

"Well, ain't nothing like a murder to get people on the phone tree at night. Anyway, I also heard there wasn't a will when the lawyer went to read it this morning."

"There must be more than a phone tree," I murmured.

"Well, I do hair for just about everybody," she said. "But from what I hear, old Ebenezer was changing up his will."

My ears stood to attention at that. "He was?"

She nodded. "You got that right." Idie Claire leaned forward now. The scent of her hairspray lingered between us. "And you know what else? And goodness knows, I shouldn't be one to gossip, but what the heck? You can't go to hell and heaven at the same time, can you?"

I shook my head. "No, and I don't know what that means."

She wiggled her eyebrows. "What it means is, from what I understand, Gilda was pretty ticked about the whole will. Ebenezer had originally put her in to inherit everything, but from what I'm gathering around town, he had changed it back to his kids."

My jaw dropped. "No. Not sweet Gilda."

"Girl, yes," Idie Claire said, tapping my hand. "Sweet Gilda got cut out. And now that will's missing, which means the lawyer's only got one week to find it. If he doesn't, everything reverts back to the older will. That's the law in Magnolia Cove."

Realization struck me like a hammer between the eyes. "And that last will named Gilda as the one who inherits everything."

She clicked her tongue. "You got that right." She leaned so close her hairspray mingled with the scent of her rose perfume. "And wouldn't you do just about anything for millions? Like commit murder?"

If I were Gilda, I just might.

TWELVE

As soon as Idie Claire and a very happy Emily left, Betty crossed to me. "I wouldn't believe everything that gossip says. She once told the town I spelled them all to be ornery so they could see what it was like to live a day in my shoes. I told her that in confidence," she grumbled.

I shook my head. "Who are you, exactly? That makes no sense. Why would you do that?"

Betty crossed her arms. "Who said I did it?"

I scoffed. "You just admitted to it."

She ignored me and crossed to the puppies. "All right, kid. Time to learn how to clean cages."

So I spent the rest of the morning cleaning cages and letting the animals out for a few minutes to run around in a bigger space. I was nervous about it at first, but they all went back to their homes happily when it was over.

The pet shop had pretty early hours, closing at five. Betty stayed with me most of the time, but she left early to make supper.

Which, with my luck, was probably bat wing cobbler or something.

Gosh, I hoped not.

I grabbed the cat carrier, locked up shop and headed out for the walk to her house, for the first time realizing my car was stuck out in the middle of the forest. Crap. Deciding I'd deal with that tomorrow, I headed down the street—

And ran smack into Todd the Policeman.

I saluted him. "Hello, Officer."

He paused, his golden eyes blazing. "Are you making fun of me?"

Oh, sheesh. Couldn't I grab a break somewhere?

"No, no, sir. Absolutely not. How're things going with the investigation?" I said, trying to steer him away from thinking I was insulting an officer of the law.

He slowly nodded. "They're going. You staying out of trouble?"

I grimaced.

"What's that look?" he said.

I shook my head. "No look. Everything's great." I felt a swell of pressure in my knuckles. I cracked them one by one, relieving it.

"Ew," he said. "That's a horrible habit."

I grinned. "Thank you."

Todd glanced down at the carrier. "Do I know that cat?"

Did he? Crap on a stick, he probably did if he visited his uncle's shop often. I clutched the carrier. This cat was my ticket out of here. I didn't need anyone else getting hold of it and scaring the poor creature to death.

"Oh no, this is a vicious stray I found out back behind the shop. Totally feral. Do not get close."

He raked his fingers through his mop of hair. "Can't you talk to it? You are the animal whisperer, aren't you?"

"Oh yeah. Ha-ha. Well, it appears that my powers of animal speak don't work as well on wild, stray, unhumanized creatures. This one seems to have some trauma also going on with it. I'm trying to figure out how to help. May take some time." I sidestepped him as he stepped forward. "Anyway, I've got to get going. I don't want to be late for dinner." I ducked around him, successfully dodging any more questions.

I brushed the back of my arm over my forehead, smearing nerve sweat across my skin. "Listen, cat, the sooner you start talking, the better. I need to get off the hook for this murder and out of this town. Too much weird witchy stuff going on for me. I like my new family, but you know, who wants to get attached? Getting attached leads to all sorts of problems—heartache, heartburn, probably diarrhea, too. Just more complications than I need."

When I arrived at what I would call home, I guess, dinner was already on the table. Amelia and Cordelia were there, along with Betty and Mattie.

Mattie sat in her own chair. Cool. I guess.

I popped open the cat carrier. The calico slowly sniffed her way out. I filled a bowl with water. "Do we have tuna around here for the cat?"

Cordelia pointed to dinner. "Just give her some turkey and dressing."

Amelia nodded. "Yeah, she'll love it. Besides, it's got turkey in it. That's pretty close to tuna."

No, it's not.

I looked at the thick spread of food. Black-eyed peas, ham, turkey with cornbread dressing. "Wow. Is it a holiday?"

Betty shuffled into the dining room, out from the swinging kitchen door. "No, this is our regular Monday meal. And I brought your cat some turkey, heard about it in the kitchen."

"Thank you," I said.

Betty smiled at me. Really smiled, like she was happy that she could help. My heart ballooned, and at the same time it constricted. A pang of longing pushed to the surface, and I quickly shoved it away.

With the cat settled, I sat down to dinner.

Amelia leaned over. "So we heard that I-Declaire-Your-Business-To-The-Entire-Town came and saw you," Amelia said.

I blinked at her, not understanding. "What?"

Cordelia poured herself a glass of sweet tea from a pitcher in the middle of the table. "That's what we call Idie Claire."

Amelia stabbed a green bean. "She's the biggest gossip in Magnolia Cove. If there's even a snippet of gossip in the air, once Idie grabs hold of it, you can guarantee it'll be all over town by the end of the day. Oh, and it'll be Bible truth, too. No joke."

I laughed as I broke open a roll. "Really? I didn't get that sense at all," I said, rolling my eyes and dripping sarcasm.

Cordelia and Amelia met my gaze. Cordelia chuckled. "I like you. You get people and aren't afraid to say it. We need more of that around here. Most of these witches are so serious," she said, waving a hand in the air. "I mean, they're witches, so magic is the most important thing to them. Obviously. But some of them are such stick-in-the-muds."

"Speak for yourself," Betty grumbled. "I know how to have fun."

"From what I understand, too much fun," I said.

Betty shrugged. "I only have the respectable kind."

Cordelia chimed in. "Anyway, what I mean is—folks around here take themselves way too seriously. They never laugh at themselves."

"I laugh at myself all the time," Betty said, scooping up a glob of dressing and plopping it on her plate. "I laugh more than anybody else in this town. I laugh longer and harder than a whole skillet of them. Just try me."

Amelia blinked at Betty. "Is that before or after you're trying to spell everyone in town to do what you want?"

I laughed and got choked on a bite. After coughing up half a lung, I found my words. "But seriously, Idie said something interesting about Ebenezer's will. She pretty much pointed a finger at Gilda, his girlfriend."

I didn't know if I should be telling them this. I didn't know if I should tell Axel this. Probably I should, but I didn't know where to find him. Course it was a small town. Someone would know where he lived.

"Gilda Goldenheart?" Betty said. "The best baker in all of Magnolia Cove? Why, she's won the apple pie contest at the Cotton and Cobwebs Festival every year. Won't share her recipe, either. Stubborn old coot."

Cordelia tapped a fingernail against her lips. "You think Gilda might've had something to do with the murder?"

My stomach tightened with guilt. "I shouldn't have said anything. I don't want y'all to get involved in this. I'm already in enough trouble as it is. No point dragging anyone else in."

Amelia reached over the table and grabbed my wrist. Concern bloomed in her eyes. "You are our long lost kin. We should have been in your life ages ago. I am not blaming anyone. All we can do from this point on is move forward. I want to help. Dang it. It's my obligation as your cousin and blood. So does Cordelia. She wants to help, too."

Cordelia smiled at me. "That's true. We do."

I studied my new cousins—Cordelia with her long, lustrous blonde hair and Amelia with her delicate features—and I realized they did want to help me. They wanted to help me as much as they could.

Amelia raised her eyebrows. "If we really want to find out what's going on, I say we go to Gilda's."

Betty rubbed her hands with glee. "Do you need me to put the town to sleep for one hundred years? Not that I would do that. I've never done that before."

I glanced around the table, a wonderful idea crystallizing in my head. "I really don't want anyone to get into trouble."

Amelia shook her head vigorously. "If you're going down, we're going down with you. We know you're innocent."

Cordelia arched a perfectly sculpted eyebrow. "What Amelia says is true. We're all in it together."

A slow smile curled on my face. It was a bad idea. A terrible idea. It would probably get me into more trouble—but hey, I was already a suspect in a murder. How much worse could my life really get?

I ignored the sense of dread quivering in my gut. "Okay, after dinner I say we head to Gilda's and see what's going on."

Lucky for me, Amelia knew just about everyone in Magnolia Cove, or Coven, as I secretly joked to myself. I sensed that Cordelia couldn't actually be bothered with the nuances of such a thing as people, but as long as one of them knew what was going on, I was glad.

"Does this make me look fat?" Amelia said. She wore slim black leggings and a long-sleeved black tee.

Cordelia shook her head. "You're already fat. How could it make you look worse?"

Amelia was as thin as a sheet of paper. I had the feeling she knew that, too. You know how we women sometimes like to be told we're skinny.

Amelia launched a pillow at Cordelia.

"Sourpuss," Cordelia said. "Of course you don't look fat. You couldn't look fat if you bathed in Crisco and deep fried yourself."

I threw them a smile. "Don't let Betty hear you say that. She might actually try it."

They laughed as we slipped from my room. "Hold on," I said. I padded back in and glanced at Mattie, who was curled up in the window seat. "Can you watch the cat?"

The calico sat on the bed, licking her paw. Her gaze flickered to me when I said that.

Mattie stretched and yawned. "Course I can. Ain't got nothin' else to do."

I grinned. "Thanks. But she can walk through doors. Pretty sure about that. So be careful."

Mattie stared at me. "That's interestin'. You might want to ask your grandmother about that. That's not a trait I've ever heard a familiar being able to do."

I nodded. "Okay, I will."

Later. Right now I needed to spy on Gilda.

I followed Amelia and Cordelia from the house. We walked down side streets with names like Sleepy Hollow, Bat's End and Cauldron Court.

"This town is so small," Cordelia said. "You can get most places easily and quickly on foot. We could drive one of our cars, but we risk being recognized. So it's probably best we just walk."

Fine with me. After about ten minutes we came to a home at the corner of two crossing streets. It was a little ways off the road, and looked about the same as all the other cottages in town—white with a picket fence, wooden bars crisscrossing the side, making it look fairy-tale-like.

Amelia rubbed her arms. "This is it," she whispered. "It's Gilda's. What should we do now?"

Cordelia pushed her cousin forward. "Well, we don't need to stand out front so that people can see us and get suspicious. We need to split up. See if we can hear anything. I'll take the left side; Amelia, you take the right."

I knew where this was going. "I'll take the back," I said.

Yellow lights burned inside the home. I saw a body move in the front, probably the living room. It looked like Gilda was pacing back and forth. Maybe on the phone.

We split up. Gilda's house was far enough away from the street and from her neighbors that I wasn't immediately concerned with anyone seeing me. I considered that lucky.

Gilda's voice drifted toward me as I took up my position. Good. She'd taken up residence in the back. I pressed myself against the siding.

"No will, honey. No idea…stolen. The kids are saying they're going to sue me for everything I've got, honey. Oh honey, I know…I don't know…Ebenezer was good to me, but the way he talked, the kids were gonna get it all…I know. Well that makes the last will the correct one unless they can find this one. Yes, honey, the last one leaves everything to me. That's why the kids want to sue me. Oh I know, honey. I know."

The kids were mad. I couldn't say I blamed them. When my father died, there hadn't been anything left. He'd had a small amount of money but not enough to retire on. Heck, I was doing my best not to bounce checks—and doing so poorly, I might add.

As Gilda continued her call, I glanced around the backyard.

A wishing well sat in front of a copse of trees.

It wasn't the plastic kind you could get from a discount store. No sirree, bricks and mortar made up this well. I walked toward it. A rope suspended down from the bar across the top. Hmm. If I had stolen a will and wanted to hide it, that seemed a likely place.

I pulled my phone from my pocket and poked on the flashlight. I shot the beam into the hole. Sure enough, there sat the bucket with a slip of paper rolled up in it.

Lighting flared through my arms. Holy jeez. This might be it.

My heart knocked against my ribs as I grabbed the handle and started turning.

SCRREEEAAAACH.

I stopped. Darn this stupid bucket. The thing was as loud as a shotgun. Or at least, that's what it sounded like to me.

I inhaled a deep pocket of air and worked the handle again.

My heart jumped into my mouth as the bucket creaked and groaned. I went as slowly as possible, ignoring the beads of sweat that popped on my forehead and slid down into my eyes and slithered along my temple.

The bucket reached the top when a tree branch snapped.

My gaze flickered into the woods. Not wanting to leave the paper, I snatched it from the bucket and took a step forward.

A black blur launched into me, knocking me on my back and the air from my lungs.

The thing flew up toward a tree. It was a shadow, a formless thing blacker than black. It moved from the pines, strutting forward.

Think.

Okay, going back toward the house would put my cousins in danger. I didn't want to do that, but they had magic. Magic that could help me.

But that shadow loomed and leaped toward me.

Fear. Fear slick as tar, black as ebony, tasting of bile and probably some sour sweet tea, surged through my body. I wanted it gone. Away.

Pressure built up inside my head.

Pressure that had nowhere to go but out.

The creature stopped floating toward me and suddenly streamed backward, away.

Had I done that? Pushed it back?

No time to think because it dropped to the ground. Shook itself off and came at me again.

So I did the only thing I could think.

I ran.

The trees were closer than the street, and I'd only just met my cousins. I couldn't put them in danger. So the trees it was.

I hurled through the brush. Branches slapped my face, tore at my pants, barbed into my side. Behind me, the crunch and snap of twigs and wood loudened. It pumped adrenaline through my body at an accelerated rate.

The trees cleared up ahead. I would be out, away from my cousins but completely alone. I was almost there when my foot caught a root. I plunged forward.

I flipped onto my back and raised a hand. The blur landed on me. I could feel it flutter and pick at me as if it was trying to yank the life force from my body. I couldn't get ahold of it; it was like trying to fight against fog. It could hurt me, but I couldn't do anything to it.

The strain was getting to be too much. I could feel the drain.

The blur grew, blooming into a blot that blocked out the nearly full moon. My breath waned. It covered me, and then the world went black.

THIRTEEN

The headache was the first thing I noticed. The next was the fact that I didn't feel like I was lying on a bed of pine needles and sticks—meaning, still stuck in the forest.

Something soft was underneath me. Like, really soft.

My eyes fluttered open.

I was on top of a sofa. Straight across from me a fire cracked and hissed. A massive TV sat in one corner. Massive as in man-sized, the kind that swallowed an entire room. A favorite of men. Also two Chippendale chairs sat squarely in the room.

Where the heck was I?

Had that black *thing* brought me here?

I rose as a body shuffled through a door at the far end of the room.

"Axel," I said, relieved.

A wave of suspicion shot through me. Why was I at his house? He hadn't been anywhere near the forest where I'd been attacked.

Or had he been?

He held out a plate of cheese and crackers. "Hungry?"

"No," I said as my stomach growled.

Traitor.

I glanced around the room. "What am I doing here?"

He nodded deeply, in a knowing sort of way. "I heard something coming out of the forest. You were tangled with a wraith. The thing knocked you out. I got rid of it, but you were unconscious, so I brought you here." He set the plate on the coffee table. "Those are nasty beasts, those wraiths. They don't come around here too often, but sometimes they do. Anyway, that's what you're doing here."

He cocked his head, and a sloppy grin, the kind that made his eyes twinkle and my stomach knot, cracked on his face. "Looks like you've got a knack for getting yourself in trouble."

"And you've got a knack for being at the right place at the right time."

"Only when it comes to you."

Silence permeated the room. It annoyed me that he'd shown up twice now. It made me feel very damsel in distress, and I was absolutely nothing like that.

I was not in distress, and I was definitely not a damsel. Damsels were weak, sad princesses who couldn't survive without a man.

I could survive without a man.

He plopped on the couch. "I got your car up and running. Drove it back to Betty's house."

My heart shifted in my chest. The cold outer layer defrosted a tad. My knees wavered a bit, and I sank down beside him.

"You did?"

He kicked his feet up on the table. "I did." He slanted his head toward me. "Don't rush to thank me."

I bristled. "Listen, I didn't ask you to do that, and I didn't ask you to save me."

"Oh, did you just want me to leave you in the forest and let the wraith suck the life from you?"

A cold chill swept over my body. "Is that what they do?"

He nodded. "Sometimes. Most of the time."

I raked my fingers over my scalp. "I could've died? What about my cousins? Did you see them?"

Axel touched my arm. A bolt of energy snaked up my flesh and pierced my heart. When I caught his gaze, my throat constricted. I swallowed a knot in my mouth and forced myself to keep eye contact, but the power of his glance made my lower lip tremble.

So I bit it. And watched as his eyes flickered to my mouth.

"Your cousins were nowhere around. The wraith vanished when I scared it off."

I sank back onto the couch.

"Why don't you tell me what happened?"

I grimaced. "My cousins and I went to snoop on Gilda to see if we could find out anything about the will. Some woman named Idie Claire came into the store today and told me that Gilda was going to be cut out of Ebenezer's will, which makes her a huge suspect. Anyway, we went over there and I found a piece of paper in a wishing well—"

"Witching well," he corrected.

"What?"

"That's what we call them here. Witching wells, not wishing wells."

I waved my hand. "Whatever. Anyway, I'd just gotten hold of the paper when that thing attacked. I didn't want to run toward my cousins because I didn't want to put them in danger. So I ran in the opposite direction."

I suddenly remembered about my power. I clutched his arm, and Axel's eyebrows shot up. I released him as quickly as I'd grabbed hold of him. "I think I used my magic. I don't know. I was so scared. Fear was running through me. I thought about getting rid of the thing, and it seemed to slow down."

"How do you feel now?"

I rubbed my temples. "Like I have the worst hangover ever."

He chuckled. "You, Pepper Dunn, are what we call a head witch."

I frowned. "What?"

He nodded. "Your magic is focused more in your head. You know, since you can talk to animals and throw a little bit of telekinesis around, that makes you a head witch."

"A head witch," I said slowly. "Never heard of such a thing."

"You'd also never heard of Magnolia Cove before yesterday."

I clicked my tongue. "That is true." My thoughts shifted to the will, and I plunged a hand in my pocket. "It's gone. The paper. What I found in the well."

Axel scrubbed a hand down his cheek. The side with the dimple. Not that I was staring or anything.

"The wraith probably took it."

"Why would a wraith want a paper?"

Axel frowned. "That I don't know."

We sat and munched on cheese and crackers in silence until the plate was gone. "Come on," he said. "Let's make more."

What, we?

I followed him to his kitchen, which was all clean lines, white cupboards, chrome and dark counters—very masculine.

Axel grabbed a handful of crackers and plated them. "It's possible that the wraith is someone in town. I haven't heard of anything like that before, but it is possible."

"What is a wraith, exactly?"

Axel pulled cheese out of the fridge. I watched as he worked quickly, smoothly to build a snack. "A wraith is an apparition, a ghost. Usually a harbinger of death."

"A harbinger?"

He winked at me. "Too big a word?"

"Shut up."

He shook his head. "I'm making fun of myself, not you. You want a beer?"

I nodded. "Yes. I would die for one."

He unscrewed the cap. "Watch out; Magnolia Cove can make you want to drink. The strangeness of it."

I rolled my eyes as I took a bottle from him. "Don't worry, Mom. I think I can handle it." I glanced at the label. "Witch's Brew?"

He nodded. "It's local."

I took a pull and said, "Never would've figured that out."

"Ouch. Who's got attitude now?"

I winked at him. "Just wait. I've got a whole suitcase of badass attitude I can unleash at any time."

He laughed. It was deep, throaty and sent a chill sweeping down my back. Our gazes met again. He stared at me from underneath thick, rich lashes. It was the sort of look that sent a shock wave straight to the stomach.

At least it did mine.

Feeling heat blaze in my cheeks, I glanced away and focused back on the cheese. "So a wraith?" I said, reminding him.

"Yes," he said, "a wraith is a ghostlike entity. Usually dead, but I suppose you work the right magic and a person could have some of the same powers."

I frowned. "Other than the mysterious and weird Rufus, who would be after me?" I realized it as quickly as I said it. "You don't think someone really poisoned my uncle, do you?"

Axel shook his head. "No poison was ever confirmed. I don't think there's anything to worry about until there's something to worry about."

I picked at the beer label. "What are you talking about? I was attacked. Don't you think that's something to worry about?"

He sighed. "That could be coincidence. You might've been in the thing's territory. I don't know."

"The paper I stuffed in my pants is gone." My eyes flared. "Unless you took it?"

Axel raised both palms in surrender. "I do not go digging in women's pants without consent."

I sniffed. "Then what happened to it?"

He shrugged. "You think it fell out when the wraith chased you?"

"Maybe. I don't know."

Axel smiled at me. "Listen, why don't we go back tomorrow, together, and search? You can show me exactly what happened."

"Okay. That sounds like a decent plan."

Axel sipped his own beer and settled it down on the counter. "Any luck with the cat yet?"

I shook my head. "None. Thing's not talking. Yet. But I took it to the shop today and let it run around. It's warming up to us. I just think it's going to take some time before it opens up. I mean, hey, it might be mute. The animal might not talk at all."

"That's true. Your uncle used to say that he couldn't talk to every animal. Not all of them have that sort of magical ability." He drummed his fingers on the counter. "But we've got to keep trying on it. It's the best lead we've got."

"And it seems like the police don't have any leads at all," I murmured. "Oh yeah, I ran into Todd today. He tried to get a glimpse of the cat. I hid her from him."

Axel's eyebrows rose. "You think he recognized her?"

I grimaced. "He might've. But I don't want her to be taken from me. Like you said, she's the best lead we've got." I snapped my fingers. "You know, I totally forgot, but Gilda was on the phone saying both of Ebenezer's kids were pretty ticked at her. And, did you know they only have a week to find the newest will? If not, everything reverts to the old will."

Axel nodded. "I did know that. Ebenezer's kids hired me before the will came up missing, but they may have had a sixth sense about the situation."

"You don't think they had anything to do with it, do you?"

He shrugged. "Anybody could've had something to do with it. I'll go by and ask them some questions tomorrow."

"Great, I'll come with you."

"You sure do like to invite yourself places, don't you?"

I shrugged. "It's my neck on the line, remember?"

Axel straightened. He crossed to me and lifted a hand. He plucked something from my hair. "Pine needle," he murmured.

He was so close I could sense the rise and fall of his chest. Body heat wafted off him and seeped into my skin. A hair's breadth apart, I wondered for the briefest of moments what his lips would feel like on mine.

I bit down on my lip and felt his gaze, hot as blazing coals, flicker to my mouth yet again. I swallowed and thought about the last guy I kissed and how much he cared about fantasy football more than me.

I did not need to get involved with anyone.

I eased back, feeling the spell between us dissolve. "My cousins. I need to make sure they're okay. I should be getting home."

Axel inhaled a deep shot of air. His chest rose and he nodded. "Yeah, I should be getting you back."

"What time is it, anyway?" I said.

Axel glanced down at his watch. "Ten."

My blood froze stiff in my veins. Holy crap, but I was in it deep.

I grabbed Axel's arm and ran from the kitchen. "Come on," I said. "We've got to get out of here."

"What's the rush?" he said.

"Don't you remember?" I said. "I've got a ten o'clock curfew."

He grabbed a set of keys from a side table. "Oh no, I completely forgot. Great. Betty's going to be waiting for us."

"I know," I said, yanking his front door open. "And I'm pretty sure that can only mean one thing."

"What's that?"

I swallowed hard before turning back to him. Dread replaced the marrow in my bones as I said, "We're going to be greeted by the business end of her shotgun."

FOURTEEN

Which is exactly what happened.

"I'm sorry I'm late," I said, gasping as I threw myself into the house.

Betty sat in the same position as the night before. Her eyes were narrow, and I swear the corncob pipe was twice as big, which if I had to guess, meant she was twice as angry.

"Your cousins came back hours ago," she spat.

Literally she spat. A wad of tobacco into the hearth. The fire hissed and crackled, burning purple for half a second.

Axel pushed himself in front of me. "Your granddaughter was attacked by a wraith."

Betty nearly tumbled from the chair. "A wraith? Here in Magnolia Cove?"

Axel nodded. "I saw it. Scared the thing off. But not before it knocked her out."

Betty settled the shotgun on the wall. She pushed a quilt from her legs and rose. She crossed to me and placed a hand to my forehead. "You feel okay. Not too hot. Not too cold."

"Can wraiths make you hot?" I said.

She tilted her head from side to side. "They can do either. Too cold means you're dead. Too hot means you're feverish."

Things I could've figured out if I'd thought about it.

Amelia and Cordelia rushed down the stairs. Amelia nearly pushed Cordelia out of her way as she spoke.

"Pepper, are you okay?"

"I'm fine. I'm so sorry I left."

"We heard a crash," Cordelia said. "Then you were gone."

"Your cousin was attacked by a wraith," Betty said. Before anyone could say something, Betty snapped. "And yes, we've got one here."

I explained about the will and that I'd found a sheet in Betty's witching well, but it had disappeared when the wraith knocked me out.

"We've got the cat," I said. "But the cat's not talking."

Axel cocked a brow. "Betty, do you know anything about how a cat can walk through walls? We followed the cat's tracks from Ebenezer's shop to the familiar store."

Betty waved her hand, and five glasses of sweet tea apparated in front of each of us. "Y'all sit down. Let me tell you about that."

Betty settled into the chair, tapped out her pipe and filled it again. The scent of pipe smoke trickled through the house. It gave my sweet tea a smoky, earthy flavor.

I kinda liked it.

In fact, I liked sweet tea so much I wanted to disagree with Axel about me being a head witch. I thought I would be a sweet tea witch instead, if there was such a thing.

"When I was young," Betty started, rocking back and forth, "I knew a witch who could shape-shift. This is different from a glamour; this is pure shifting. Some of the power involved in it can be dark. For you, Pepper, that means the witch would've used evil spirits to help her change."

"And did you sell her the herbs at the chemist store you owned?" Amelia asked.

Betty scowled. "Little miss, my job was to supply people with what they needed, not to ask questions."

"That's a yes," Cordelia said.

Betty snapped her fingers and Cordelia's tea vanished.

"Ah," Cordelia said.

Amelia gripped her glass hard. "I'm not saying anything bad."

"Good." Betty cleared her throat. "Thing was, the shape-shifter got into something bad one night, something so bad it killed her. When they found her familiar, which was a cat, the animal had tracked through the mess and wound up in the attic of a neighbor three houses down. Same thing. The cat had appeared to walk through walls."

"But how?" I said.

Amelia pressed a finger to her lips. "Don't interrupt if you want to live."

Betty shook her head. "I've never killed anyone."

"You've never *not* killed anyone, either," Amelia added.

Cordelia smacked her head. "That doesn't make any sense."

Amelia smiled pertly. "But it was a good rebuke."

Cordelia rolled her eyes. "So how did the cat do it?"

Betty sucked hard on the pipe. "Simple. A surge of power from the witch's death gave the cat the ability to walk through walls. At least for a little while. That's the same thing with your calico upstairs. The animal may have witnessed the murder. When Ebenezer died, a magical surge allowed the animal to be able to do things it wouldn't normally be able to."

"Hmm," I said, "that only answers the question. It doesn't get us any closer to solving the murder."

Axel rubbed his hands down his thighs. "Right. But at least it's good to know. Thank you for the tea."

We all rose. Axel stared at me and for a moment I felt like I was supposed to walk him out. I guess since I'd invited him in, that was the only way to go about it.

"I'll see you to the door."

He nodded. "Yeah, and I can show you where your car is."

"Oh, thanks. I need to find a mechanic, I guess, get the whole thing looked over. Get all her parts fixed."

"I'm sure he can fix your parts," Betty said.

I froze. "What?"

She winked at me. "You know, get your parts fixed. Lubed up. Oiled down."

I. Was. Mortified.

My stomach clenched, sweat sprinkled my palms and heat flushed my body from my neck down to my toes.

Axel waved a hurried good night, and I pushed him through the door. A warm summer breeze picked up the scent of honeysuckles. The aroma trickled up my nose, and I breathed deep.

He pointed to my old jalopy. "There she is."

"What do I owe you?"

Please don't make it be much.

Because I had, um, five dollars to my name. I hated to tell him, but I'd have to pay installments for probably the rest of my life at the rate I was going.

"You don't owe me anything," he said.

I smiled, nodded. The wind kicked up, wedging a stray hair between my lips. I saw Axel move to brush it aside.

I beat him to it.

Yes, my heart pounded. Yes, dear goodness I wanted him to touch me, but clearly I had a terrible track record when it came to choosing guys.

And obviously a man called Mr. Sexy around town probably has a reputation for loving women and leaving them.

I did not need that drama in my life.

He held my gaze for a moment. Nerves flittered in my stomach. I didn't know what to say, so I figured why not bring up embarrassing stuff?

"Sorry about my grandmother. She's clearly very awkward around people."

"What?" he said.

I almost groaned. Great. Now I had to explain what I meant. "You know, the whole joke she made at the end."

"What joke?"

Was he kidding? I might die of embarrassment if I have to say it again. "You know, the whole oil thing."

Axel shook his head. His dark hair brushed the top of his shoulders. "No idea what you're talking about."

I cocked my head back. "You're joking, right?"

He laughed. "Yes. I am. Give that lady a chance to make an innuendo, she'll take it."

"I know," I nearly shouted. "And she's the one who was sitting with a shotgun when we got back."

He placed a hand over his heart. "I know. I thought I was a dead man."

"Me too," I said, shoving his shoulder playfully.

We paused. The air stilled, yet the pressure of our energy built up around me. "Well, I guess I'd better get back inside. I've got a shop to open tomorrow."

He shook his head. "No you don't. The familiar shop is closed on Tuesdays. Most of the shops in town are. It's kind of a witch thing."

I fisted my hands in excitement. "Seriously? I have the day off?"

He nodded. "Yep."

I joked when I said, "Well, maybe I'll run into you tomorrow night. Perhaps you'll be three for three and save me from another danger."

The light in his eyes faded. Axel's jaw clenched, and he said in a dark, hoarse voice, "No. You won't see me tomorrow night."

Chills swept down my spine at the harshness of his tone.

"Oh. Okay."

He raked his fingers over his jaw and said, "I'd better get going. See you around. Good night."

"Good night," I said feebly.

With that he left.

I couldn't help but wonder as I made my way back inside the house, what I'd done wrong. But as much as I wondered that, I also wondered what it would be like to kiss Axel.

I had a feeling he wondered the same thing about me, too.

I WOKE up the next morning to Mattie and the calico curled up on my bed. Before I had a chance to stop myself, I found my hand stroking Mattie's head and my other fingers scratching the calico under the chin.

What was happening to me?

"Hi there, Sweetie," I said, giving her a name other than calico cat.

I got up, showered and met the rest of the family downstairs for breakfast. Both cats followed me.

"So," Amelia said, scooping a clot of eggs onto her plate, "Cordelia and I were thinking we'd help you figure out your magic today. We've both got the day off, too."

I bit my lower lip. "Funny thing, Axel figured it out."

Betty's eyebrows shot to heaven and back. "You'd better watch out for those oil-lubing men."

I fisted my hand. "Yeah, and can you please try not to embarrass me in front of him?"

A slow smile curled on Betty's lips. "Spoken like a true granddaughter of mine."

Cordelia curled her fingers around a glass of orange juice. "What's your power?"

I cringed. "I don't know if it's right, but Axel called me a head witch."

Amelia's fork clattered to the table. "A what?"

I scooted eggs around on my plate. "I don't know. Last night with the wraith, I got so scared that something happened. It seemed to slow down, get thrown back. No power left my hands, like with y'all when you do magic, but it did happen."

Betty cackled. "Holy smokes! A head witch. I declare, this is a great start to the day. A granddaughter of mine, a head witch."

I frowned. "Is that bad? Is it bad that's what I am? Maybe I'm not a head witch. Maybe I'm more of a feet witch."

Cordelia flicked her napkin onto her empty plate. "A head witch is one of the most powerful witches there is."

My jaw dropped. "What? Really?"

Betty grabbed Cordelia's wrist. "Yes, but you need training. Lots of training." She pointed a finger at all of us. "And no telling anyone what she is"—she looked at me—"what *you* are. Word gets out about it, we'll have all kinds of witches bothering us."

"Why?" I said. "I don't understand. Y'all know I don't know squat about this whole witch thing. You have to help me."

Amelia, having picked her fork up, cleared her throat. "Because a lot of times head witches can heal others. Do things with their head magic that others can't do."

"Oh." I laughed. "Don't worry. I have no clue how to even do magic, other than listen to animals' voices. So don't worry about me."

"Great," Betty said. "Keep it that way. I believe after breakfast the girls have a treat for you."

I felt my eyes spark at the mention of a surprise. "Yes? What's that?"

A trip home?

Even as I thought it, I realized that Magnolia Cove was growing on me, murder investigation and all.

Cordelia slung her purse over her shoulder. "We're heading to Castin' Iron."

I dabbed my mouth with my napkin. "Is that the place where witches go to get those skillets they ride instead of brooms?"

Amelia leaned forward, a wide smile splitting her face. "That's exactly right. And guess who's about to be a brand-new rider?"

I gulped. "I guess that would be me?"

Betty nodded. "You got it, kid. Have fun and don't break your neck because I won't be able to fix it. I can fix a lot of things, but necks aren't one of them."

"Oh," I said, surprised. "That's good to know."

FIFTEEN

Before we headed to Castin' Iron, my cousins and I dropped in at the pet shop and fed and watered the animals.

Amelia pulled one of the kittens from the cage and stroked it. "You know, I don't know why I never got a familiar. They're all so sweet and wonderful."

"Because you're allergic," Cordelia said as she slipped fresh newspaper under the puppies.

Amelia lurched forward. "Ahchoo." She placed the kitten back in the cage. "Case in point."

"I'm allergic, too," I said, "but it seems to be getting better the more I'm around them."

Cordelia tucked a strand of long hair behind one ear. "So, do they, like, talk to you all the time?"

"Yes, we do," one of the parrots squawked.

"Play with me," one of the puppies yelped.

I laughed. "Pretty much. One of the puppies wants you to play with him," I said.

Cordelia reached in and pet all the pups. "Can you tune it out? All the chatter?"

I nodded. "It's getting better. It's sort of a low hum unless one of the voices breaks through." I looked around the shop, and satisfied that the animals were okay, I brushed off my hands and said, "All right, who wants to ride a skillet?"

Castin' Iron was the place to go if you wanted any kind of witchy tool, I quickly found out. They specialized in cast iron and had a small forge in the back. Set off as a separate building on the main stretch of Bubbling Cauldron Road, the front was all rough-hewn unpainted boards, while the inside flourished like a home—bouquets of dried flowers were pinned to the walls, fresh-cut flowers dotted the tabletops, along with sitting benches.

Cauldrons of all shapes and sizes peppered the space. Large, squat ones with deeps bowls hung from the ceilings, short slim ones sat on the floor and a teetering stack lined the wall behind the counter.

And of course there were the skillets. Long, thin handles, as long as ones on a broom, with oblong-shaped pans floated in the air.

"Oh," I mused, "so that's how you can ride them. They're much bigger than a regular skillet."

"Come in, come in," came a voice from the back. A short little man wearing a leather apron and clothes slashed with singe marks toddled in. "Come in," he said again. "Take a look around. We make the finest cast-iron skillets for riding anywhere you go. And if you want a custom one, we can do that, too."

"That's not true," came another voice. "He hasn't done custom in years. Takes him too long."

A short woman with long white hair popped up from behind the counter. I jumped back.

The man swept over to the woman. "Stop it, Theodora. You don't know. I made a custom skillet for riding just last…year."

Theodora smirked at us. "Harry likes to think he fills orders fast, but he don't. If you were waiting on him to make you a riding skillet before you could marry your prince, your prince would be dead by the time the skillet was finished, and you'd be dead and buried in the ground."

Harry threw up his hands. "Stop it, woman! These are customers."

Theodora looked us up and down. "And customers I plan on

keeping by telling them the truth. Take a look around," she said to us. "See what you see. Let me know when you want to try one."

Amelia and Cordelia pointed at me. "She's the newbie. We've both got ours."

Theodora's eyes sparkled. She clapped her hands as she shuffled out from behind the counter, her white hair floating around her.

"Oh, a new witch! I love new witches. Come, come, dear. You get to try a skillet for the first time."

Harry stepped up. "My family started riding skillets a couple of hundred years ago." He pulled one of the skillets down and thumped the bottom of the pan. "They hold up better than wood. And look, the cushion on this one is velvet, though you can have whatever cushion you want."

"That," Theodora said, poking the air, "is the one custom quality that don't take long. We can have that fixed within a day. That's because I do it," she said, shooting Harry a contemptuous look.

"It isn't a competition, woman," he shot back.

Theodora smirked. "Speak for yourself. But go on, give it a ride. We've got a whole course out back for you to learn on. Pick a skillet, any skillet."

I glanced around the room, feeling completely overwhelmed. "But are they heavy?"

Harry chuckled. "Not heavy at all. Here."

He released the one in his hands, and the skillet simply floated in air. Magic. Right when I started getting used to it, something completely unexpected would happen, like a skillet hovering in air.

A cast-iron skillet that should weigh a ton.

I bit my bottom lip and started to curl my fingers around it.

"Wait!" Theodora said.

I dropped my hands.

"Sorry, dear, didn't mean to scare you, but you're that Pepper girl, aren't you?"

Word travels fast. "Yes, ma'am. I am."

She clapped with glee once again. "You're the new Mistress of Familiars. We've been waiting for you!" She squeezed my shoulders.

"So glad you've finally come to us. Oh, what would this town do without you? Your uncle was wonderful at putting familiars with their witches, but women are always better at that sort of thing."

Harry rolled his eyes. "So the woman says."

Theodora shot him a shut-it look. "I'm bringing my granddaughter into your store tomorrow for her first ever, and you know what? I might just get one myself!" She giggled like a girl. "It's been years since I've had a familiar, and oh, I love them so. Can't you just see it? I'm a skillet witch with my skillet familiar. How wonderful."

I smiled. "Of course. Bring her in. I'll be there."

I said it as if I accepted the store as part of my life now. My stomach still twisted at the thought of staying, but not as much as it had before.

Theodora pushed the skillet toward me. "Try it out. See what you think."

I curled my fingers around the elongated handle. The metal hummed under my touch. I rocked it up and down, feeling the weight.

"It's so light," I said.

"Yep," Cordelia said, sinking down onto a chair. "Light as a feather."

"Please don't say, stiff as a board," I said.

Amelia laughed. "You're one step ahead of us."

I ran my fingers over the bumps and grooves of the iron. It looked exactly like a skillet you could cook with, only the pan was stuffed with a cushion for sitting, and of course the thing was ungodly long.

"How does it work?" I said.

"The magic is in the iron," Harry said proudly. "I'm a flying wizard by birth, so that's the magic I pour into the skillet. The power in the skillet feels your magic, they mingle and you go." He zoomed his hand toward the sky. "That's the simple beauty of it."

"Simple beauty of something," Theodora grumbled. "Come on. Grab the one you want and we'll go outside."

I held on to the first one Harry had given me and followed her through the crowded, dark store that seemed to have more nooks and crannies than a cave, until we reached a back door. Theodora slung it open, revealing an obstacle course of sorts.

Ropes and orange cones marked out a path. The ground under the path was padded, which I thought was strange.

Theodora clapped me on the back. "Now, all you need to do is get on and go."

I slung one leg over. It was awkward, I won't lie.

"Pull the handle until your tush rests on the seat," Theodora prodded.

So I did, though my bottom rested wobbly on the thing.

"That's it," she said. "Now, ease down. The skillet won't drop you. It'll hold."

I sat like she said.

"Cross your ankles behind you; it makes it easier."

Next thing I knew, my ankles were crossed and I was floating on a cast-iron skillet. Pretty sure I threw my head back and gave a roaring witch cackle to go with it.

Harry laughed. "She's getting it." He came up and lightly touched the handle. "Now, all you need to do is think where you want to go. Every skillet here knows the path. So focus on it and go forward."

With my hands clamped tight and my ankles locked, I shifted my gaze to the course and thought, *Go through it*, or something like that. It was probably simply *go*, which the skillet did.

Without me.

The skillet zipped out underneath, leaving me flat on my back on the ground. I blinked, the wind knocked from me and my eyes wobbling around.

Theodora popped into view. "Oh, that one didn't like you."

"What?" I said, confused.

Harry popped in the other side of my line of sight. "Sometimes a skillet doesn't like the rider. Nothing personal. Let's get you another one. See if it'll be better."

Amelia ran up. "Already done. Here, Pepper, try this one."

Cordelia helped me up, and I rubbed my bruised tush. "It looks the same as the other."

"They all look virtually the same," Theodora explained, "but the personalities can be different, like with anything."

I took the skillet from Amelia and sat again. This time the going was a bit better. I glided down the course, the ride smooth and starkly fun until I got about halfway down.

That's when the skillet knocked me off.

But luckily this time I had the padding. So that's why the course was padded. Clearly I wasn't the first person this had happened to.

"Of course not, dear," Theodora said when I grumbled about it. "Almost everyone gets knocked off."

Amelia raised her hand. "I got knocked off."

"Me too," Cordelia said. "Those skillets are picky. I had to come back three times before I found the right one."

I cocked a brow. "Really?"

She nodded.

Harry took the last skillet away and handed me a fresh one. "In fact, in all my time I only remember two people who haven't been knocked off a broom."

"That's correct," Theodora said. "Only two."

I eyed the new skillet skeptically before taking it. "What's this one like?"

Harry pointed to the black cushion studded with silver knobs. "Oh, this one hates everyone. We'll see how far you get, and that'll tell me which way to go."

My jaw dropped. "It hates everyone and you want me to try it?"

Theodora nodded. "Come, come. Dear, sometimes a little hate tells us a lot about a person."

"But I don't hate. That doesn't even make sense."

"We mean the skillet," she said. "If it allows you to stay on for only a second, that'll help Harry figure out which way to go next. If it keeps you on longer, then we know more. Very simple. Should've put you on this one first, but we didn't think of it."

"I thought of it," Harry said, "but I didn't want to get yelled at for suggesting it."

I rubbed my bruised rump and said, "Do I really need to do this?"

Amelia laughed. "We all have skillets. You don't have to get one, but a lot of us have them. We ride around at night, laugh at the moon, work magic."

Cordelia pushed a curtain of blonde hair from her eye. "No, you don't have to. It's just fun to have one."

I decided to give it one last shot. Figuring I wouldn't stay on the skillet very long anyway, what could it hurt to try?

I wrapped my hands around said evil skillet and took off. I expected to be bounced off quickly, and as I wound my way around the path, a bubble of glee buoyed up in my chest.

I found myself smiling. And laughing. And completely enjoying the ride. In the back of my mind I waited, though, wondering if I would be kicked off at any time. It was possible and highly likely, and I figured the end was coming any moment.

But as we rounded the bend and returned to the drop-off, where Amelia, Cordelia, Theodora and Harry waited, all of them with big grins on their faces, I realized that I'd achieved something wonderful and surprising.

"Way to go," Harry said, clapping me on the back. "I knew you could do it."

Theodora thumbed her chest. "I knew it first. Knew it from the moment you sat on that devil there."

"No, you didn't, woman. I knew it first!"

I patted the air. "Now, now. I think you both realized it at the same time."

Theodora took the skillet from me. "This is yours. First time this boy has let anyone take him all the way around the course. I'd say it was meant to be. We'll wrap it up for you."

My delight soured as I realized I had about five bucks to my name. "But what about payment?"

Theodora sniffed. "We'll trade; how about that? The skillet for my granddaughter's familiar."

Cordelia leaned into my ear and whispered, "They're expensive. That's a good deal."

I stuck out my hand. "Done."

Harry shook it, and I followed them back inside. As Theodora fussed the skillet into brown paper, she mumbled, "Yes ma'am, only two folks I can remember have made it around the bend without being thrown off once." She looked up, smiled. "So your ride was normal, though the skillet you ended up with was not."

Curious, I said, "Who were the two people?"

Harry shuffled past. "The first I'm sure you can figure out. She's short with curly silver hair and has attitude to spare."

I laughed. "You must mean Betty Craple."

Theodora nodded. "Your grandmother could stare down a rabid raccoon and send the thing scurrying, tail between its legs."

Harry leaned into my view. "Better still, she could give the Loch Ness monster the stink eye, and it would swim off screaming for help."

When our laughter quieted and Theodora handed me the paper, I said, "And who was the other person?"

As she walked us to the door, she leaned over. "It was an event that surprised the heck out of me. Young boy, full of power, conquered the very first skillet he sat on. He didn't live in town at the time, but he does now. You might know him."

I crooked my head toward her. "Who was it?"

"Name's Axel Reign."

I nodded. I did know him, indeed.

SIXTEEN

Sunlight practically glowed off the sidewalks when we stepped back onto Bubbling Cauldron. I shielded my eyes, letting them adjust. My gaze swept up and down, settling on Police Officer Todd talking to a man about half a block down.

Actually, they weren't talking, more like arguing.

"Who's that?" I said, nodding toward a round man with dark, thinning hair.

"That's Bob Bubble," came a voice from the side.

My head swiveled in the direction of the mysterious voice. Idie Claire smiled brightly at me.

"Hope I didn't scare you. I wasn't trying to. I was passing by and heard your question. Since you're already under suspicion for murder, I didn't figure you meant Todd the Policeman. The one he's talking to is Bob Bubble."

I narrowed my gaze. "Who's that?"

Cordelia opened her mouth to speak, but Idie Claire cut her off. "He's the town bookie."

"Town bookie?"

Amelia nodded. "We have some witch sports that folks bet on. My guess is Bob's in trouble with Todd."

Idie sidled up. She poked her nose right in my face. "Or it's the other way around. From what I hear, Todd likes to bet."

My brows shot up. "He does?"

"Yep. Heard it from his best friend's wife. Imagine that—a policeman owing a bookie. Never heard anything like it in all my life. But, that sort of gambling is legal here, so that's just how it goes." Her gaze raked over my hair. "Let me know when you want to schedule a cut. I'd love to get you in my chair."

My own gaze drifted off her teased mop of hair. I gulped. "Thanks. I'll let you know."

As soon as she was gone, Amelia leaned over. "She might be a huge gossip, but she does the best hair in town. It's an experience like no other."

"I'll remember that."

As we walked back toward the house, I sneaked a glimpse at Todd. His cheeks puffed red. He was mad about something, and as much as I didn't want to believe that he was a gambler because, I mean, policemen were supposed to be so straight and narrow, it was hard not to believe it when our eyes met and he looked away, guilt flooding his face.

We returned to the house. When I got upstairs, I put the skillet in the corner.

"We're taking that out tonight, you know," Cordelia said, popping her head in.

I quirked a brow. "We are?"

She nodded. "Yep. There's nothing like a summer ride on your skillet in the middle of the night under the full moon. It's amazing."

I shrugged. "Okay. I'm game."

"It'll make you feel more like a witch than anything else," Amelia said, floating by.

I smiled as they both left me to the quiet of my room. I found Sweetie the Calico buried in a pile of dirty clothes in the closet, sound asleep.

"She hasn't talked," Mattie said, stretching from her slash of sunshine in the window seat.

"Hmm. I'm hoping that'll change. We be nice to her, hang out with her, she'll come around."

"You should take her on your ride tonight. Real familiars love skillet rides."

Laughter barked from my throat. "You're kidding, right?"

Mattie shook her head. "I used to go with your mother all the time."

I pulled my hair up into a ponytail. "Okay. Well, I'll see if she wants to come. Thanks for the suggestion. Meanwhile, I'm going for a run. I don't suppose you want to follow me on that?"

Mattie stretched. "No. Running ain't my style, but nappin' is."

I grinned. "That's what I thought."

I opened my closet, which luckily had been stocked by Cordelia and Amelia with better clothes than 1970's rejects. I fished out running pants and a shirt and pulled on a pair of sneakers and set off for a run.

I passed Betty at the hearth. She crumbled some dried herbs into her cauldron. "Is that lunch?" I said.

She shook her head. "No. This is going to be bath salts."

I frowned. "It smells like meat."

Betty grinned widely. "Good. That's what I was hoping for. Hamburger Heaven. That's the name of it. Gonna bottle it and sell to my friends."

Okay. "I thought lavender was a better scent for bath salts."

Betty stirred the pot. "I'm starting a trend."

Of insanity?

"I'm going for a run. Is there anything you need while I'm out?"

Betty nodded. "We could use milk. And none of that goat stuff. Regular old bat's milk will do."

My eyes flared. "What? Have I been drinking bat milk?"

She waved a hand. "Nah. I'm kidding. Just pick up a gallon from the corner store. Tell 'em to put it on my tab."

"Okay."

Whew. Thank goodness. She almost had me vomiting in my mouth there. Good thing that didn't happen.

I set out the front door at a slow jog. My brain had been full of fog since I arrived. Let's face it, a crap-ton of things had been thrown at me. I needed to compartmentalize, get it all together. My brain shifted back toward the wraith's attack.

I had been attacked.

I needed to tell someone. Like, perhaps the police because, I mean, the thing had stolen the piece of paper from Gilda's well.

These are all things Officer Todd needed to know, and I had to tell him. I didn't know where the police station was, but it couldn't be that hard to find. I mean, Magnolia Cove was a small town. I jogged past Bubbling Cauldron to a series of municipal-looking buildings set back from the road.

I knew I smelled like sweat, but who cared? I slowed to a walk, stretched out my calves and thighs and pushed open the glass door. I told the desk sergeant who I was there to see and he called Todd to the front.

The officer smiled when he saw me, his golden eyes shining. The guilty look from earlier gone.

"This is unexpected," he said. "You here to admit guilt?"

To be honest, I couldn't tell if he was joking or not.

"No," I said. "I want to report that I was attacked."

Todd's hand curled around my arm. "Are you okay?"

I nodded. "I'm fine. But I wanted to file a report."

Todd glanced around the station filled with bustling bodies. It was funny. The officers in Magnolia Cove didn't dress like regular police officers—you know, the whole *Van Helsing* thing. But they did have badges pinned to their shirts.

It was a gold shield with a silver broomstick over a black cauldron. Simple, sweet, to the point.

Todd guided me down the hall to what I assumed was his office. "Come in. Tell me exactly what happened."

So I did, even explaining that I was in the woods near Gilda's property. His face changed from concerned, to dark, to bemused.

"I'm not going to ask you what you were doing on private property."

"I was lost," I said. "Got lost wandering around Magnolia Cove. Whew. I mean, there are a lot of twists and turns in this town. Anyway, from what I understand, it was a wraith. I don't know if you have a list of people capable of turning into a wraith, but I thought you'd like to know."

He steepled his fingers in front of his face. "That is good. I'm sorry you were attacked."

I shrugged. "It's just one more thing in this crazy ride we call life, right? But anyway, any leads besides me on who killed Mr. Goldmiser?"

Todd grabbed a stack of paperwork and started riffling through it. "We've got some things we're looking into."

But from the way he avoided my glance, I had the strong feeling that there were no other leads. I was it. Which meant, if I didn't act fast, I wouldn't have to worry about whether or not I should stay in Magnolia Cove.

Because I'd be locked up in the prison caves with no hope of escape.

SEVENTEEN

Apparently, riding during the full moon was a big deal in Magnolia Cove. Like a huge deal. Half the town met up in one spot and took off on a tour of the town and the outskirts. My goal was to stay far, far behind so that if I fell off, I wouldn't be embarrassed.

I might break my neck, but at least I wouldn't poop my pants from nerves.

A girl can hope, right?

We met up at Coven Park, which was just past the residential district by downtown. There were at least a hundred witches, including myself and my cousins. Betty didn't come, as she said she had other things to do.

"She never goes out with us on the full moon," Amelia said to me on the way over. We had walked, by the way.

"Maybe she's a werewolf," I said. Amelia and Cordelia exchanged a suspicious look. "Is she?"

"Of course not," Cordelia said. "Come on, we need to pick up the pace or we'll be late."

As I said, the park was packed. We found spots in back, near the playground. I put the cat carrier on the ground, deciding I'd open it up when we got closer to starting. I peeked inside. Sweetie meowed at me.

Well, I guess the lines of communication were officially open.

A few other witches were milling around, and I noticed one was a man with short copper-colored hair. I realized he was one of Ebenezer's children.

A pang of sadness crept over me. I'd found his father's body, attended the will reading but hadn't given this poor guy my condolences.

Which was what a good person would do.

"I'll be right back," I said to my cousins.

I approached the man. I knew he and his sister had hired Axel, but I didn't know any more than that.

"Excuse me," I said.

The man glanced up from his phone. Streetlamps surrounding the park lit up his eyes, which matched the burnished tones in his hair.

"My name's Pepper Dunn. I wanted to tell you how sorry I am about the loss of your father."

He quirked a long, sculpted brow. "You knew him?"

I twisted a strand of hair nervously. I had my skillet in one hand, the hair in the other. "Well, I, um… I, um…"

His eyes flared with understanding. "You're the one who found him."

I gulped. "Right. But I didn't do it. I didn't kill him."

A smile flickered on his face. "I know you didn't. Why would you? You wouldn't inherit the money. Money that's rightly mine and my sister's," he said bitterly.

I wanted to know everything so badly, but I didn't want to push too hard. But what the heck, I might not get this chance again. "The new will was missing, I understand."

"My name's Dean, by the way."

"Nice to meet you."

"Likewise." Dean rubbed the back of his neck. "My father shut my sister and I out of the will years ago. Said we were greedy, ungrateful children. He left everything to Gilda, bypassing us completely. See, it all happened after he and my mom divorced. She didn't let him see us, so that's why he had such a bad opinion of us."

"I understand," I murmured.

He picked at the stem of his skillet. "It took years to prove to him otherwise. We finally did, near the end." He choked on tears. "And he changed the will. Told us he did so. But now that's gone. And who's the person who inherits based on the previous will? Gilda."

"She seems like such a nice woman," I said.

"Oh, don't let all those 'oh honeys' fool you. That woman's a shark. Ask anyone who's worked the baking contests with her." He leaned forward. "Folks have suggested that she sabotages their entries. I don't know if it's true, but that's what they've said."

"Hmm. And now there's only a few days to find the new will," I said.

"Yep. If it's not found, the previous will gets used."

I smirked. "And the older one? Does it list you at all as beneficiaries?"

Dean rubbed the heels of his hands in his eyes. "No. It lists some other folks, cousins, and Gilda but not us."

"Is there anyone else you can think of who might've done it? Might've wanted to hurt your uncle?"

Dean shook his head. "No. Gilda's the one. I've told Axel, I've told Todd but no one wants to believe it's her."

I thought for a moment. "And did you see the new will? The one that named you and your sister to inherit everything?"

Dean blanched. "No. I never saw it. But my dad promised me that's what he'd done. Why would he lie?"

Why indeed?

I thanked Dean for his help and rejoined my cousins just as a slim woman with a whistle around her neck blew the heck out of it and said, "All right, y'all ready?"

Excited murmurs buzzed through the crowd.

"Do we have any newbies?" she said.

I did not want to raise my hand. I hated, I mean hated being singled out for things.

Amelia glanced over and saw that I wasn't going to volunteer information. She raised her own hand and said, "Yes. There's a newbie."

The coach woman's gaze raked over the crowd, so I tucked down into the handle of my skillet. "Okay, newbies. These are the rules. Stay with the coven of riders. Don't veer away. No tricks unless you're a pro at them. We don't want anyone getting hurt. And when we go over the Cobweb Forest, be sure to stay out of it. Bad things live in there. Everyone got it?"

I nodded, and Amelia answered for me, "We've got it."

I placed Sweetie in front of me, on part of the padded seat. She sat comfortably, as if this was something she was used to.

I exhaled a deep shot of air. Okay. This might be all right after all. Part of me was worried that she'd fall off the skillet, but Mattie had insisted, saying a familiar used to riding would stay on no matter what. That's what they did.

So here we went.

"Everyone up," the coach yelled.

I readied myself. Personally I didn't know if my talents were up to the test of riding with this group, but Amelia and Cordelia seemed to think so, and I trusted them.

I trusted them. The thought made my stomach clench.

It was true. They were the only family I had, and they'd welcomed me with open arms. I hadn't realized how withered and small my heart had become over the past few years since my dad died, but it had.

I mean, my last boyfriend cared more about fantasy football. That should tell you a lot about the kind of love I had been inviting into my life.

The wrong kind.

I was ready for the right kind, and it was all happening now, in Magnolia Cove.

The skillet lifted off the ground. Sweetie balanced like a pro. Still, I curled one hand around her, as I didn't want anything to happen.

We soared over the park and toward downtown. Wind whipped

my hair. Magic hummed and thrummed in the air, buzzing from my chest all the way to my toes.

"What is that?" I said to Cordelia. "That magic?"

Her lips coiled into a smug smile. "That's the magic of the ride. It's everyone's magical energy. It's amazing, isn't it?"

I nodded. "It feels like we're touching power. Real raw power, the kind that creates and destroys."

"You are," Amelia said, laughing herself past me. "It's a heck of a ride."

It sure was. The pace was slow at first, which I was grateful for. Cordelia and Amelia had worked with me all afternoon, making sure I could take off and land. They told me over and over that once you got the right skillet, the rest was easy.

So it was. We glided on air currents of magic over houses that dotted tree lines and hills that I didn't know existed in Magnolia Cove.

"We're coming up on Cobweb Forest," Amelia said. "Cordelia and I always play tag around here. We've done it ever since we were kids. Hold tight and go slow. We'll be back."

"Are you okay by yourself for a few?" Cordelia said.

I nodded. "I'm fine. This is amazing."

They jetted off, and I paused, soaking in the glowing moonlight and glancing down into the forest. I understood why they named it how they did.

The full moon cast streaks of light that looked like webs over the trees. A silvery glow bloomed on the leaves. It was gorgeous.

Something black flashed below. We were maybe twenty feet above the tops. The rules were not to go down into the forest. I wasn't going in there, but I wanted to take a closer look. Cordelia and Amelia were still zigzagging ahead of me.

I eased the skillet down toward the trees.

The black flashed again.

A cold chill ripped through me. Sweetie reared back. She hissed, turned and launched herself at my chest.

Claws ripped my shirt, startling me. I lost my focus, lost my balance. The skillet careened down. I tried to tug it up, pull it back toward the sky, but Sweetie was clawing her way up my shirt to my throat.

The pain ripping up my skin took all my focus as the skillet crashed through the trees. Branched snagged my hair, sliced my clothes.

We were going down, falling into Cobweb Forest. The one place I was told not to go.

And the darn cat was still clinging to me for dear life.

The skillet plowed through a line of dirt. I braced my feet, helping slow our trajectory. We came to a stop inches from a large pine.

I heaved out a breath and unhooked Sweetie from my neck. I wasn't so sold on the name Sweetie anymore. More like Death Wish. Yeah, I might reconsider her name.

I got her off me. She pushed her fragile body into my chest. The cat shook. Clearly the black thing, whatever it had been, had scared her to death.

That still didn't give her the right to almost get us killed.

Yes, Death Wish and I would be having a conversation if we ever got out of here.

"Okay, cat," I said. "Calm down. It's going to be okay."

I pulled her off my chest and sat her on the seat. I got off the skillet, brushed my pants and rose. I needed to take a look and make sure nothing was broken on the thing before trying to take off again.

Any crack, any fracture, and I wouldn't ride it. No one had said anything, but I didn't know if the magic would hold.

I was running my thumb down the handle when an eerie howl broke the night air. It sounded like a wolf. It was loud, close by.

I shook my head. I knew I'd regret doing it. I just knew I would, but I needed to know what I was up against. I couldn't simply ride off without seeing.

Of course, there was the black thing to take into consideration, too. The shape we'd seen in the forest that had scared the holy heck out of Sweetie Death Wish.

Yeah, I kinda liked the ring of that.

The howl had come from behind a towering hedge row.

A hedge row? In the middle of a forest?

That didn't make sense.

I left the cat on the skillet and padded over as quietly as I could. The hedges were thick, full. I walked to one side and saw that another row sprouted up alongside. I followed until I came to another knuckle or corner of hedges. I followed that to another bend.

I realized I was standing in front of a hedge square. In the middle of the forest someone had taken the time and care to plant a barricade made of hedges.

Why?

My heart hammered as I parted the bushes. They were thick, so very thick. Another row of hedges butted up inside the first. I kept on and found another. There were hedges inside of hedges. I pushed on and on. Finding more and more.

Surely they would have to run out.

I caught a sliver of moonlight seeping through the greenery. There it was. An opening.

I pushed through as my foot caught the bottom of the hedge.

I pitched forward, landing splat on top of a clear patch of dirt.

A low growl filled my ears. I glanced up to see a wolf. It was three times as large as a normal dog, with a chest like a wooden drum. Saliva flung from its jaws as it snapped.

I scrambled to a seated position and backed up toward the hedge. The animal's black silhouette popped in the moonlight. One crunch of those jaws and my bones would shatter. No doubt about that.

My heart pounded. I pressed back into the hedge as the wolf leaped straight at me.

EIGHTEEN

The creature lurched forward, but it couldn't move. My heart jackhammered; sweat sprinkled my brow. My brain filtered every bit of information as quickly as possible.

Why hadn't the wolf reached me?

Then I heard it.

Metal scraped against concrete. I squinted and noticed a chain extending from a concrete slab to the animal. A thick steel collar wrapped around its neck, keeping the creature from breaking free.

The wolf snarled and chomped, but the chain held it fast. It couldn't reach me.

"What in tarnation are you doing here?"

My gaze swiveled over and landed pointedly on Betty.

I stumbled back. "What's going on? What is that thing?"

The wolf continued to snap and lurch. Betty cocked her head for me to come over. I kept a wide berth, scraping my back along the hedge.

She aimed the shotgun at the animal and said, "That *thing* is a werewolf."

My body jerked and trembled. "A werewolf? What do you mean a werewolf? We're witches. I can accept witches. Hold on. I can mostly accept witches. It's still a pretty hard concept to grasp, but now you're saying that's a werewolf?"

Betty nodded. "Full moon plus werewolf equals death to others, so I guard him every full moon."

My eyebrow. "Him? Who is it?"

Betty's jaw snapped shut, reminding me of the creature's. "I'm not allowed to say. I'm assuming you were on the skillet ride."

I rubbed my tush. We'd hit the ground hard, and I had a feeling one cheek would be black-and-blue by tomorrow. "I have the calico cat with me. We saw something dark in the forest. It spooked her, and we came crashing down."

Betty's gaze raked over me. "You'd better get on out of here. 'Fore anyone notices you disappeared."

I nodded meekly and brushed dirt and pride from my sleeves. After pushing back through the hedges, I found both cat and skillet unharmed. I climbed on, and we lifted from the forest, leaving me with more questions than answers.

THE NEXT DAY was business as usual at Familiar Place. I went in, fed the animals and started to get the hang of matching familiars with their witches. I hated to admit it, but it was actually fun.

Don't tell anyone.

Part of me felt like I was living the best life, this new witch life. If only I didn't have a murder hanging over me, then things would've been perfect.

Sweetie Death Wish still wasn't talking, though she would curl up in my arms and purr. I figured one thing at a time wasn't that bad.

I finished my work at the pet shop and did manage to sell Theodora's granddaughter her very first familiar mouse. I never would've thought that's what the kid would've pegged, but a nice brown house mouse ended up being her match.

I had just locked the door for the day and had popped some of Carmen's jelly beans in my mouth when a voice caught my attention.

"How's your car working?"

I glanced up. A tendril of crimson hair drooped in my face. I tucked it behind an ear while catching a glimpse of Axel Reign. It had only been a day since I'd seen him, but the effect he had on me—the tingling, heart knocking in my mouth, heat rising in my cheeks—hadn't diminished one speck.

I swallowed the knot in my throat along with the jelly beans. "To be honest I haven't tried it. I've been too busy. And now I have a witch skillet and can ride that. So why would I ever need my car again?" I said, laughing.

Axel chuckled. His shoulder-length hair was pulled back into a holder. The waffle-patterned shirt he wore hugged his muscles in all the right bulging places. I licked my lips, and his gaze flickered to my mouth.

Talk about tension.

"I'm glad you're making it okay," he said.

I remembered the conversation I'd had with Dean and stepped forward. "I spoke to Dean, Ebenezer's son, yesterday. He said they still can't find the will. Do you think it's in the pawnshop?"

Axel scrubbed knuckles over his cheek. "It might be. Worth checking out."

I smiled brightly. "Do you still have a key?"

He groaned. "I suppose this is the part where you tell me that since it was your idea, you have to come check out the store with me."

I nodded enthusiastically. "That's exactly right. You managed to take the words out of my mouth."

"I must be psychic."

"More like in touch with the universe in sort of a new-age-crystals-and-lavender kind of way."

He laughed again. It was throaty and made my chest constrict. "I'd say I'm just really good at reading people."

I couldn't hide the bright smile pushing onto my face. "So that means yes?"

He nodded. "Come on. Before it gets dark and people notice the lights on in the shop. Let's get it done."

We walked down the street. He placed a hand to the flat of my back. Intense heat spread over my skin.

My gaze slid to the side. "Are you feverish? You're really hot."

He laughed. "No. My temperature's higher than most folks. Come on, let's go around back."

We entered the shop. I unzipped the cat from her carrier and let her sniff around, see if maybe being back in the pawnbroker's store would get her talking.

"I guess the first place to start is the office?" I said.

"I'll follow you," Axel said, nodding.

Axel opened the filing tower and started rummaging through the papers while I took the desk.

We shuffled through paperwork. Mostly that turned out to be receipts, invoices—nothing important. The basic stuff you'd expect to find at any business.

"I went on a moonlight skillet ride last night," I said. Filling silence with idle chatter tended to be one of my strong suits, and I was proud of it. Man, I could talk to you about the weather all day.

I heard Axel's fingers drum through the sheets. "Oh? How was that?"

Besides my cousins and maybe Idie Claire, though her friendship was questionable, Axel was the only other person I'd really connected with since I'd been in Magnolia Cove.

I hesitated in telling him—felt my knees quiver. But I still needed to purge to someone besides Betty and her shotgun.

"I fell into Cobweb Forest."

His fingers stopped dancing over paper. My gaze shot up. Axel leveled his stare on me. His blue eyes darkened, becoming an ocean of anger. "Cobweb Forest is a dangerous place."

"I know," I said, turning my attention back to the papers at hand. "It was an accident. Something spooked the cat, and we crashed in the forest."

He returned to riffling. The sound of sheets shuffling filled my ears. "Are you okay?" he said.

"I am. I was. I saw something; I don't know what it was. Some black shape. It was almost like the wraith that we saw the night before. Then it got even stranger. When I got inside the forest, I found—this is going to sound crazy—a werewolf. Betty was guarding it."

Axel's jaw twitched. I wasn't sure what that meant. I didn't know if he knew about the creature. But I reckoned if anyone in town would know, it was him.

"I've heard rumors of such a thing," he murmured. "Should stay out of that place. It's dark, dangerous."

"I know. It was an accident. I didn't mean for it to happen. Magnolia Cove is so strange and wonderful. On one hand I feel like I belong; on the other I feel like something here might kill me."

I laughed nervously. An instant later Axel's hands were on my shoulders. "I know how this place may seem. I didn't grow up here either. I came later. My powers are limited. I'm a wizard, among other things, but I understand what you mean about Magnolia Cove." He smiled at me, a glimmer of amusement flashing in his eyes. "I know it doesn't help that Rufus is out there waiting for you. Oh, and you were found at the scene of a murder."

"Your powers might be limited, but not according to Theodora at the skillet place. She said you rode a skillet without falling off your first try."

"I guess my wizard blood runs deep, though that's not my main ability."

"What's your main ability?"

Axel's hands squeezed my shoulders. Darkness loomed in his eyes. My lower lip trembled. I didn't know why. Fear? Anxiety? Trepidation?

"There are things about me that are too hard to talk about."

I nodded. "Okay. Listen, you don't have to tell me anything. It's not my business. I'm just here to find some papers, look for a will, escape from Rufus and go back to Nashville." I clenched my hands in frustration. "I don't even know what Rufus wants, so I figure it's going to be a battle of the fittest, or of the strongest, or whatever."

Axel chuckled. "You might be right about that, but I hope not."

My head jerked up at the sound of a key turning a lock. Axel snapped his fingers, and the lights in the office popped off. He grabbed my hand and pulled me underneath the desk.

Though it wasn't black in the office, it was still somewhat dark. Dark enough that if someone glanced inside, they wouldn't be able to see us hiding beneath the desk. But if they wanted to use said desk, the gig was going to be up so high you might as well rocket off into outer space.

Axel's shoulder pressed mine. Both of our rear ends were totally sticking out, but there was no time to position another way.

The back door opened, and someone shuffled inside. The desk faced the hallway. The big old grand mahogany was solid top to bottom. There wasn't even a sliver to peek through and see the shoes of whoever had entered.

But I could still hear.

Footsteps padded toward the front room.

I could feel Axel's warm breath on my cheek. The scruff of his chin grazed my temple. My heart pounded as someone shuffled things in the front room. Axel turned his face toward me. His lips brushed through my hair.

Fire ignited my skin, thrumming in my core.

Every inch of me cracked and fizzled as if my nerve endings extended from my skin, bleeding out.

The shuffling continued as if someone was searching. Perhaps they were searching for the exact same thing we were—the will.

The sounds from the front room grew louder, and Axel turned his face more in my direction. I wondered if he could feel my heart drumming my chest.

A minute later the footsteps padded down the hallway and out the back. The lock clicked, and I released a heavy sigh.

"One more moment," Axel whispered.

"We don't need to be found here," I murmured.

"Just wait. In case they come back."

"We need to stop whispering."

"I'm not the one who keeps talking."

I quirked a brow. "You just did."

"They might hear us," he whispered.

"Then stop talking."

Axel grabbed my wrist. "Okay, stop."

I stopped. I think it was the combination of his skin on mine and the hushed tone, but I zipped my lips and waited what felt like forever, but was probably about thirty seconds.

"I think it's safe to get out," I said.

"Wait one more minute."

"They're not coming back."

I felt him adjust, turning toward me. "Trust me, I don't want to be here any more than you. I really don't want to be here."

"I don't want to be here either. It's cramped—"

"Not to mention hot."

Boy, he wasn't kidding. The temperature from his body practically made the cubbyhole hum. But it wasn't just the heat; there was something more. Tension building up, blowing out and coming to a head. I could hear it in my own breathless voice, sense it in the gruff tone of his.

"I'm sweating," I said. Yeah, I know it wasn't sexy, but it was true. Give me two more minutes tucked under the desk and I'd have an armpit of BO that could knock down a bulldozer.

Literally, if the bulldozer could smell and stuff.

I felt his finger brush against my leg. A bolt snaked up my thigh and straight to my girl parts. "I'm hot, too. I just want to make sure…"

"I think we've made sure. We don't need to be found under the desk," I whispered.

"We don't need to be found anywhere. I have a key, but only a few know about it. Todd doesn't. If he knew I had access and was walking all over his crime scene, he'd be mad."

I turned toward him and felt my lips brush his chin. My skin sizzled at the contact. "I don't like this any more than you."

"I'm cramped."

"Not to mention stifling."

"I keep bumping into you."

"I have no air."

"It's the worst position to be in."

Heat crackled in the tight space. I felt Axel's fingers graze my arm. "We should get out. I think it's safe now."

I couldn't move. The closeness of him, the fire churning in my belly—both things paralyzed me.

I licked my lips. "Then we should leave. Get out."

"Not before I do this."

His lips found mine. My skin popped, fizzed. The air crackled and hissed as if the very atmosphere was made of fire. Magic ripped through my chest like a ghostly wraith, and I felt my power churn and bubble.

My mind swam; my brain fuzzed and dimmed. I couldn't think. I couldn't process. All I could do was feel.

And boy, was I feeling.

Then as quickly as it started, it ended.

And the tension began.

"Sorry, I shouldn't have done that," Axel said. "I don't want you to think I was trying to take advantage of a situation."

The lights snapped back on, and his features swam before my eyes. I laughed nervously and wiped my bottom lip. "Time to get out."

"Yeah," he said.

I exited first, giving him a great view of my rear end. This was the South and ladies first still applied; there was no getting around that.

Axel smoothed his hair, and I tugged on my T-shirt. "Listen, you don't know anything about me," he said. "You just moved here. I don't know what came over me."

I quirked a brow. "Animal attraction?"

His eyes darkened. "Yeah, something like that."

I pumped my hands nervously. "Listen, it's okay. We all make mistakes. I just got out of something, and I'm not really looking to jump right back in. You've probably got a girlfriend on the side. I mean, they do call you Mr. Sexy in town. I'm sure that's not for nothing. So, let's just chalk this one up to wrong place, wrong time and a nerve-racking situation and keep going. I'm okay. Are you okay?"

His jaw dropped the more I talked.

"I talk when I get nervous," I admitted.

"There's nothing to be nervous about," he soothed. "Pepper—"

My heart soared at the sound of my name on his lips. *Bad heart, bad heart. Stay down, girl. Don't get me all excited about this guy who's clearly about to kiss and break my heart.*

"Pepper," he repeated. "You know, that's really a great name."

"Thanks. Apparently food names run in my family."

He nodded. Pulled his hair from the holder and retied it. "What I was going to say is that there's no one else. I haven't dated anyone in a while. I'm not very good at it, and there are things about me…things I can't share with anyone and I wouldn't want you involved in."

"Oh? You troll the dark Web selling illegal cheese? Is that it?"

He laughed. "No. I wish it were that simple."

I crossed to him, patted his arm like a robot trying out touch for the first time. "It's fine. Really. Just a kiss. No biggie. We're still friends."

Something sparked in his eyes. I couldn't tell, but it looked like a hint of disappointment. "Yeah. But don't think this means I'm going to let you tag along any more than you already are."

I shrugged. "Come on. Let's go grab Sweetie Death Wish and get out of here."

He frowned. "Sweetie Death Wish?"

I laughed behind my hand. "Yeah. That's what I named the cat. Sweetie because that's how I call her, and Death Wish because, well, she nearly got me killed in the Cobweb Forest."

He smiled. "I like it."

I padded from the room to the front of the store. "Sweetie, where are you?" I glanced around, looking to where I'd kept the cat, but she wasn't anywhere.

"Do you see her?" I said to Axel.

He shook his head. "No." He peeked behind chairs, behind statues, furniture, clocks. "Where's she hiding?"

A slow, sinking realization seeped into me. I checked for her cat carrier, but it was gone, too. "Axel, I don't think she's hiding anywhere. I think whoever came in here stole Sweetie Death Wish."

NINETEEN

"Somebody's been kissing. I can tell."

I stood on the front porch. The guard-vine sniffed me curiously. Axel stood on my right. Betty blocked the front door, arms barred over her chest.

How could I not have been mortified? I was a twenty-five-year-old woman with a new life, including a grandma, and in a flash I'd been reduced to a sixteen-year-old coming home from prom.

Worse, Amelia popped her head through the open door. Her gaze swung from Axel to me. I could practically see the glee dancing in her eyes.

"No one's been kissing," I said.

Betty traced her jaw with one fat thumb. "That's a lie. I always know when kissing's been going on."

Okay. Change of topic was in order in, like, yesterday. "Sweetie Death Wish was kidnapped. Is there a way to find her?"

Betty glanced from me to Axel before inhaling a deep sniff. "Come in. Let's talk about it. But I don't want any more kissing going on in the house."

My cheeks flamed so hot I was pretty sure my temperature was

101. I couldn't look at Axel to read his expression. I was so mortified the only place I could look was the ground.

I tromped inside and plopped my purse to the floor. "We were in Ebenezer's shop trying to look for the will."

Betty sat in her rocking chair. "That's where the kissing happened, isn't it?"

From her position leaning on a wall, Cordelia tucked away a smile threatening to take over her face. Amelia simply squeaked with laughter.

At the same time, even though I was being raked over flaming coals fueled by moonshine and magic, I realized that Betty cared about me.

My heart jumped at that. Happy that my little makeshift family cared for me.

But then what if they vanished like my dad when he died? What if it was all taken from me again?

Perhaps some risks were worth it.

Perhaps.

I cleared my throat. "The calico was taken in the shop. Is there a way to find her? Figure out who did it?"

Betty steepled her hands and said, "Maybe. Let's eat on it and think."

Axel placed a hand on my shoulder. "I've got some things to do—"

Betty aimed a finger at him. "You're staying, mister. You're not allowed to kiss and ditch."

Axel's jaw dropped.

"Besides," Betty said. "We might need your advice on the matter." She glanced at me. "Wizards often have a different take on these things. Come on. I made pork chops with fried okra and creamed potatoes."

Mattie ventured down from her spot in my room for dinner. We sat around, and Betty took her attention from me and speared it into Cordelia.

"How's that boyfriend of yours? The one who won't commit?"

Cordelia turned a deeper shade of red than I had. I know because

I'd glanced at myself in the mirror as I walked by. But I don't think Cordelia's red was from embarrassment. I think hers came from anger.

"Zach's great, thank you very much."

"So great he won't put a ring on it?"

Cordelia cringed. "He's got a lot to do with his studies and whatnot." She glanced at me. "My boyfriend is gone a lot. He's studying magical history, so it takes him to different places."

"Girl in every port," Betty said.

Cordelia snapped her fingers. A photo of a man with short dark hair and an arm wrapped over Cordelia's shoulder popped into view.

She smiled widely. "That's Zach."

"He's very handsome," I said.

"Don't anybody worry about me over here," Amelia tittered. "I've got a whole slew of beaus lined up."

"No, you don't," Betty said. "You're too desperate. Men can smell it a mile away."

Amelia flushed.

"Wow. Okay. So is this what mealtime is normally like?" I said to Betty. "Have y'all been going easy on me or something?"

Betty smirked. "I'm looking into men for Amelia. I've got something going for her." She snapped her fingers, and a rolodex of names, pictures and hobbies appeared. It looked like an online dating profile.

Not that I would know anything about that.

I didn't, but maybe I'd just trolled one or two sites in my lifetime.

"Oh no," Amelia said. "Here we go again."

"What?" I said.

Amelia shook her head. "She's trying to fix me up."

Betty poked an image of a young man with buckteeth, big glasses and a too tight T-shirt on, standing in front of a sailing boat.

"He's handsome," Betty said.

Amelia made gagging noises. "He's got zits all over his face, and that photo is clearly magicked to look like he's standing in front of a boat."

"Says he's got a sizable 401K," Betty countered.

Amelia turned to me. "Didn't you need help figuring out what happened to the cat?"

I nodded as I saw Axel cough into his hand. I grabbed the plate of mashed potatoes, creamed if you're from the country, and passed them to him.

"Yes. We were hiding in the pawnbroker's shop. Someone came in and took Sweetie Death Wish. We need to find out who."

Betty picked up a pork chop and sucked at the bone. "It's tricky when you live in a magical town. Everyone else has magic, too, and can use it to cover their tracks, erase that they were ever there. I can concoct potions using herbs to influence people, but unless someone left an obvious clue to their presence, it's hard."

She licked grease from her fingers. Then she pointed the chop at me. "If you're really a head witch, and all signs are pointing to that, you're the most capable of discovering the truth."

I pushed okra around my plate with my fork. "How?"

Betty glanced over at Axel. He coughed into his hand and said, "No one really knows everything a head witch is capable of. You can move things with your mind, a telekinesis of sorts, and you can also communicate with animals. Head witches may be able to even read a regular person's mind, but that takes a tremendous amount of strength and ability."

I frowned. "How do you know so much about all this?"

He shrugged. "I come from a long line of head witches. It's a hard talent to have. Hard to control. That's the main thing you have to focus on with it."

Betty dragged her pork chop over a line of grease pooling on her plate. She took a big bite and spoke while chewing. "Your mother showed signs of being a head witch. Lots of signs, though she chose to ignore them. I tried to train her, but she wouldn't listen."

I shrugged. "Well, I want to be trained. I don't want all this stupid knowledge and stuff inside my head. I want it out in the world where it can be used."

"That's a good thing. After dinner, let's start your training. Kissy-face boy," she directed at Axel, "I need you to stay and help. Then you can go back, do what you need to do. You've got more experience with head witches than I do."

I really didn't understand the big deal, but I was happy to play along. We finished up dinner while Betty flipped through more pictures of wizards, trying to get Amelia to bite on at least one of them.

Cordelia pushed her food around her plate, barely saying anything. I had the feeling the whole bit about Zach not committing had bothered her more than she let on.

We cleared the table, washed the dishes and pushed the furniture out of the way.

Axel paced the room. "From time to time, you may feel a push, a pressure on your head. That means it's time to release some of your magic. It may come in the form of a headache. That's when you know. You may also get a headache after you use your magic, like last time. But that should get better as you go."

I nodded. "Okay. What do I do when I get a headache?"

Betty waddled over to the fire, stoked it. "That's when you need to release your magic. Keep it from building up."

Axel nodded. "Exactly."

"So what's the best way to do that?"

"Move things," Axel said. "Use the magic and push."

I sank back onto one hip. "What?"

Betty rolled her eyes. "Catch this."

She flung the poker straight at my face. The tip burned red-hot. Fear surged from my head to my toes. I threw out power, fear. Flung it at the stick.

And it shot across the room in the opposite direction, clattering to the floor.

I heaved out a breath. "I can use it when I'm afraid, but when I don't need it, I'm not sure how to use it."

Betty rubbed her hands together. The poker lifted off the floor and floated back to her hand.

"Thanks for almost killing me with that thing," I said warily.

Betty placed her fingers on the tip. "It's not hot. It wouldn't have hurt you."

I flashed a look to Cordelia, who nodded. "Our grandmother may be a lot of things, maniacal among them, but she's telling the truth. She wouldn't have hurt you."

I guess I was relieved. "Okay. But how does this help me find Sweetie Death Wish? So what? I can protect myself if a flying can of whoop-ass is coming at me, but otherwise I'm out of luck."

Axel's gaze narrowed. "It helps because a head witch, theoretically, can open their mind and listen. You can hear where the cat went. The two of you bonded. The animal/witch owner bond is strong in a head witch. You may be able to discover where she is."

"So might you," Betty said to Axel.

His expression went blank.

What was I missing?

Amelia crossed to me, took my hands in hers. "It may take a while to figure that out about your power, but I know you can do it. I know I'm only a couple of years older than you and our mothers are out exploring the world on a lifelong vacation, but I remember a bit about her magic."

Tears glistened in my eyes. "You do?"

She nodded. "Aunt Saltie, I used to call her."

Cordelia rubbed her arms together. "Sassafras was too hard for us to say, so we called her Saltie."

Amelia smiled. "I think it's where your name, Pepper, may have come from."

My heart jumped to my mouth. "It is?"

Amelia shrugged. "I like to think so. But Saltie could use her little bit of head witch magic and give me the candy I wanted before I ever told her about it."

Cordelia laughed. "Yeah, she was amazing at that. Always knew what we wanted before we did. Good old Aunt Saltie."

Betty nodded. "She was only part head witch. Come here, kid."

I walked over to Betty. She took my head in her hands and tugged it down. She inspected what felt like every inch of my scalp. "Looks like you're mostly head witch. It'll take time to figure out your powers. My guess is Rufus knows what you are, too."

I pulled my head away from her clawlike grip. "You think?"

Axel nodded. "That's why he's stalking you. Until you've got your power under control, you need to stay here."

I scoffed. "Well, don't worry about that since last time I left, he attacked me."

Betty frowned. "We could always put a cloaking spell on you. That might keep Rufus from finding you."

Hope sparked in my chest. Then it extinguished. "I'm a suspect in murder, though, right?"

"Hopefully not for much longer," Axel said.

Then he smiled. Really smiled at me. His blue eyes nearly seemed to spark. Little creases formed in the corners of his eyes, and that dimple of his—*grrrrwww!* I just about wanted to poke my tongue in it, see how deep it formed.

Was that weird?

If it was, I was in serious lust and full of weirdness.

Some animal things couldn't be helped, I guess.

"We'll keep working on it," Axel said. "But I need to go. I've got some things of my own to work on."

"I'll walk you out," I said.

"No kissing," Betty called out. "I'll know if you do."

Dear Lord in heaven. How did I end up here? With a woman who knew when I'd been kissed? What the heck else might she know? Or at least be able to figure out?

Probably best not to know the answer to that.

I walked him out the door. The honeysuckles filled the night air again. "Thanks for helping me," I said.

We drifted off the porch to the sidewalk. "Yeah. Anytime. You need to practice, and like I said, I had a family of head witches on my mom's side of the family. I can help."

I quirked a brow. "Just your mom's side? What about your dad's?"

Axel coughed into his fist. "Listen, about earlier today…"

Did he just ignore my question? I shoved the realization from my head as quickly as it flashed in my brain. "No biggie. Neither of us want anything. Look, I was just walking you out to be nice. I wasn't looking for another kiss." I backed up.

He grabbed my hand. Fire shot to the tips. "And what if I do?"

I gulped down a hard knot as I stared into the turbulent ocean that was his eyes. "Oh, um. I don't know…" Yes, call me a chicken. "Betty said we shouldn't. Right? She'll know, my life will be hellish…"

He smiled. This time it was bitter. "I know. She'll keep you away from me, and I don't blame her."

He started to release my hand, but I grabbed his. "What? I don't understand."

Axel shook off the darkness and smiled, this time genuinely. "Look, practice. I'll stop by tomorrow, see if we can pinpoint the cat's whereabouts."

"Okay," I mumbled. He started to walk away. "Axel?"

"Yes?"

"That thing earlier about using my head witch powers—does something bad happen if I don't? I kinda got a sense back there…" I shivered. "I'm sure it was nothing, but I wanted to ask."

Axel gritted his teeth. "You have to use the power, now that you have it. Otherwise…" He stopped, flicked his hand.

I hugged my arms. "Yes? Otherwise what?"

He scrubbed a hand down his jaw. "Otherwise a buildup of power can kill you."

TWENTY

Axel assured me I would be fine. "I have to tell you the truth," he said. "It wouldn't be responsible if I didn't."

We sat on the porch steps, our shoulders touching. "Did that happen to anyone in your family?"

He nodded. "It did. Happened to my aunt."

My heartstrings tugged at that. "I'm so sorry."

He shook his head. "She ignored her power. Didn't appreciate it for what it was until finally the pressure killed her."

"That's horrible."

He stretched out his legs. "It wouldn't have been so bad if she'd recognized the signs, but sometimes the magic a head witch has can make them a little looney."

I planted a perfect facepalm on my head. "Great. So if I don't die from my power, I'll go crazy instead."

Axel chuckled. "I think you have to have underlying mental illness for that to happen. You also have to ignore everyone when they tell you you're going a bit off the wall, then hole yourself up in your house or move out to the swamp, where you end up a hermit. Those are also factors."

I laughed. Besides the fact that I figured that's what had happened to his aunt, I couldn't help it. Axel chuckled along right beside me.

I knuckled a tear away. "It's really not funny."

He nudged me with his shoulder. "No, it's not." He tipped his head back to glance at the stars. "Ever wonder how much power they have over us? The stars and what they foretell?"

I watched as a comet sprang across the sky. My breath caught at its beauty. "I guess for the most part I think I control my own fate. Why? Do the stars hold sway over you?"

His face did that dark thing again. "More than I could ever say."

It was my turn to nudge him. "Okay, Mr. Mysterious. I think that's what I'm going to tell the ladies in town to rename you. That's more appropriate than Mr. Sexy."

He did that deep throaty laugh that reminded me of velvety whiskey tumbling over ice. "It's a stupid name. They don't know me, but they gave me a nickname that reflects my outside and not my inside."

"Wow, deep."

He shook his head. "What matters is on the inside, not the outside. I've learned that the hard way."

I leaned back, locked my elbows. "Everyone's gotten their heart broken by a looker."

He shook his head. "It's not that."

"More Mr. Mysterious."

He smiled, flashing his gorgeous dimple. Axel slapped his knees and rose. "I've got to get on. Things at the house don't clean themselves, all that. But listen, I'll stop by in the afternoon. See if I can help you with the cat."

I cracked my knuckles. "You don't think someone would hurt her, do you? I mean, what if someone stole her so that they could silence her?"

Axel traced a finger over my shoulder. Even through cotton, his touch made me shiver. "I don't think so. Let's just focus on finding her, okay? Not think about all that other stuff."

I nodded, shuddering as he disappeared down the darkened street.

My heart sank. I hoped above all else that nothing happened to Sweetie Death Wish. Because if it did, I was directly to blame. After all, it was my fault that she'd been in the store to begin with. I only hoped we found her in one piece, safe and sound.

∼

THE NEXT MORNING as I was getting dressed, I noticed Mattie jump down from her window seat.

"Any helpful hints on how to reach out to Sweetie Death Wish would be helpful," I said as I yanked on a pair of black leggings.

"Well, I wouldn't call her usin' that name. I'd use her real one—Sprinkles."

I did a double take. "What? Sprinkles? How do you know that?"

Mattie yawned. "She told me."

I paused in my hyperventilating attack. "Okay. Last time you said the cat wasn't talking."

"It's not like we became BFFs or nothin'. She just told me her name."

"And why are you only telling me this now? Knowing her name could've helped us bond."

"She didn't want you to know."

I yanked the legging so hard I lost my balance and landed on my rump on the carpet. "Why didn't she want me to know?"

Mattie stretched out her paws and clicked her claws on the top of the seat.

"Don't do that, please. You have a nice scratching pole downstairs."

"Sorry. I'm only a cat. I forget."

"But why didn't Sprinkles tell me her name?"

"She's quiet. I'm sure she would've told you in her own good time."

"And now she's been stolen."

"You'll find her." Mattie jogged over to me. "I'll help. I'll come with you today. See what we can stir up."

Mattie followed me to work. Betty promised to come by, bring my lunch. She said it was her special frog's legs and rice. Part of me wondered if she was going to make stew out of the eyeballs. Don't ask me why that thought occurred to me; it just did.

I got to the store a few minutes early and fed and watered the critters. Yes, I was taking to calling them critters in my head.

"Where's the little Sweetie?" one of the parrots said.

"She was stolen."

The animals broke into an uproar. Pups barked, kittens mewed and even the snakes in the aquariums hissed.

I patted the air to settle them. "As soon as we can, I'm going to find her." An idea blazed in my head. "Maybe y'all can help me."

"We will," they shouted. "We will."

The day breezed by. Even though it was Thursday, Familiar Place was hopping. More cars pulled into the parking spots, filling downtown to popping.

"It's getting close to the weekend," Mattie said. "A lot of witches come for a few nights to get away from the city."

I quirked a brow. "Oh?"

Mattie spoke while cleaning her face. "There's Hocus Pocus Hollow not far from here."

"What's that?"

"An area of town rich with magic. They have the Prophecy Pools where you can bathe and swim, and also the Conjuring Caverns, where sometimes covens come to work important spells."

"Interesting. Well, hopefully they'll need familiars."

The witches did. The shop crackled with energy. When Betty showed up with her famous frog legs, I didn't even get a chance to eat. By the time I was ready to lock the doors that night, I was spent.

This being a head witch thing was more exhausting than I thought. I was about to close up when Axel swung inside.

The air quickly thickened with tension. My gut twisted as I gazed into his blue eyes. Our gazes locked for several breaths before I inhaled a shot of air and looked away.

I mean, you could've sliced and diced the tension with a samurai sword. Or a bowie knife.

"Hey," he murmured.

"Hey, yourself," I said. "Any leads on the case?"

He shook his head. "No. And I still don't know who came in yesterday and took that cat."

I pulled my hair back from my face and twisted it into a messy bun, poking a pencil through it to secure the bundle.

"Were you busy today?"

I sank into a swivel chair behind the counter. "Were we ever! I sold so many animals that I'm going to have to start restocking. I'm down to two puppies."

Axel smiled. "That's good. Do you need me to show you how to reorder?"

"Yes, please."

We discussed that for a few minutes. He showed me a catalog my uncle had kept. The whole time we were digging through it, he was leaning over me, smelling of pine and musk. My heart raced, and heat rose in my cheeks. I nearly fainted, but I did manage to jot down a list of all the animals I needed.

"How do they arrive?" I said.

Axel grinned. That dimple peeked out. "By magical carrier in a truck. Same-day delivery."

I fisted the air in victory. "Awesome. Now we just have to find Sprinkles."

He frowned. "Who's Sprinkles?"

I rolled my eyes. "Oh, that's Sweetie Death Wish's real name. Mattie told me." I rose. "I have an idea about how to find her."

Axel crossed his arms and leaned his hip on the counter. "How?"

"I use the animals. They help me focus." I glanced nervously at him. Axel's expressionless face made me think it wasn't going to work. "I don't know if it's a good idea or not. It may be worthless."

He shook his head. "No, I think that's smart. Let's try it."

I grinned brightly. "Great. Only thing is, I don't know how."

He chuckled. "All ideas and no execution. First thing I suggest is to ask the animals to help you concentrate on her."

Hope flared in my chest. "Great idea. Okay, animals, I need you to help me focus on Sprinkles. We've got to find her."

"What does she look like again?" asked a puppy.

"I thought her name was Sweetie Death Wish," squawked a parrot.

"Do we have to?" said a kitten.

"Sheesh," I said to Axel. "It's like trying to wrangle rats doing this."

Mattie jumped to the counter. "Let me see if I can help."

She scrambled up to the top of the kitten cage, and she started yelling like a drill sergeant. "Okay, you lazy lags. Sprinkles and Pepper need our help. Y'all need to get it together, or I'll make sure each and every one of you ends up with a little girl who likes to give you baths in fingernail polish!"

The animals stood to attention.

I brushed my hands together. "Well, I think that did it." I glanced around the still room and said, "I've never done this before. I don't even know if it can help, but we need to find Sprinkles. I want all of you to help me focus on her. Supposedly I'm a head witch, and if we can pool our power together, maybe we can figure out where she is. It might not work. I don't know, but it's worth a shot."

No one said anything. I took that as it was go time. So I placed my fingers to my temples because that's what psychics always did in movies, and I focused on Sweetie Death Wish—I mean Sprinkles.

The air pulsed and throbbed. I focused on the cat, throwing out head power, or whatever I had, to try to pinpoint her location. I figured if I could just get an image in my head of where she was, or a word, or something, we'd find her no problem.

But nothing was coming. Static filled my mind. The air buzzed. It hummed. Energy tendrils throbbed in a thousand directions without focus, without leadership or vision.

Then I felt hands over mine. My eyes fluttered open. Axel stood behind me, the cups of his palms covering my knuckles and fingers.

"Breathe," he murmured.

I closed my eyes and did as he said. Immediately focus flooded my body. It was like an invisible thread lashed Axel to me. His magic bled inside me, warm and bright. It filled me with joy, happiness, but at the same time I sensed something dark, deep inside. A hint of power peeking out behind a curtain. I reached for it, trying to decipher what it was.

The blip vanished, hiding from me.

Whatever secrets Axel wanted to keep to himself, needed to stay that way. It was none of my business until he revealed whatever truths he wanted.

A bright flash filled my brain. The magic of the animals and myself converged, splintered off and came together in one brief moment.

Then vanished.

I blinked my eyes open.

The kittens stirred. The pups whimpered.

It was from the parrot box that the words came. One of the macaws, stark feathers, intelligent eyes, said, "Sprinkles is at the house with the witching well."

Axel's hands left mine, taking with them all heat from my body.

I blinked and girded my stomach. "So now we know."

Axel raised a brow. "Know what?"

I gritted my teeth and said, "Gilda took Sweetie. And it's up to us to get her back."

TWENTY-ONE

Mattie jogged on home to tell Betty about Sprinkles while I hopped in Axel's truck. "You have two vehicles?" I said.

He chuckled. "Why do I get the feeling you're judging my choices rather than praising them?"

I shook my head. "I'm not judging. Not at all. If you want five vehicles, go for it."

His gaze slanted over to me. "I only have two. Pick-ups haul things. Sometimes I need to haul."

"Bodies?" I said.

He smirked. "I'm a PI, not a coroner."

The cabin smelled like him—piney and musky. I inhaled deeply, hoping he didn't notice. Don't worry, I stopped myself from jumping in his lap and plunging my nose in his shirt, though don't think I didn't run it by myself first to make sure it wasn't a great idea.

It wasn't.

I didn't think he'd appreciate my own appreciation for him.

We reached Gilda's house in about two minutes. Axel stayed on the main street, pulling off a few houses down.

"So what's the plan?" I said.

He paused. "I'm thinking."

"Why don't we just walk up and knock on the door, tell her we know she's got the cat and to hand it over?"

He frowned. "You know, not a bad idea. Let's do it."

We got out of the truck and headed down the sidewalk. A dim light glowed from the back of Gilda's house. I could hear her talking.

"Now hold still, honey; this won't hurt a bit."

Then I heard Sprinkles meow. I mean, it was probably Sprinkles. Hard to say. I didn't know her well enough to say it was her meow. Let's face it; I'd spent more time with animals this week than I had over the course of my entire life.

Hand-to-heart truth, y'all.

I shot Axel a concerned look and took off in a sprint. I rounded the back of the cottage and found Gilda in the backyard with Sprinkles.

Sprinkles was sitting on a wooden table. Fear raked across her little kitty face. She was glancing up at Gilda—

Who was holding knife.

The blade glinted in the moonlight.

Gilda arched the blade up in the air. It was obvious what was going to happen next. The steel tip would come down, right on Sprinkles.

Anger and fear filled me. I wouldn't be able to reach the cat in time to save her. Magic flung out from me.

The knife flew from Gilda's hand, disappearing into the trees beyond the house.

"Stop," I shouted. "Don't touch that cat."

Axel ran up to Gilda and pinned her hands. "Pepper, get the cat out of reach. Animal cruelty is a serious offense in Magnolia Cove, Gilda. You know that."

Gilda glanced at both of us, confusion on her face. "But honeys, you don't understand."

Sprinkles jumped into my arms when she saw me. I pulled her to my chest and dug my nose into her fur. When I glanced up at Gilda, anger flashed in my core.

"No, you don't understand. We know all about you, Gilda. Getting rid of the cat who saw you commit Ebenezer's murder? Is that it? I can't believe I thought you were a kindly old woman. Now I know you're nothing but a cat killer along with a human killer."

"But honey, I didn't do it," she pleaded.

"Save it for the cops," I said.

Wow. It felt really satisfying to say that, as if I'd wanted to say it my entire life.

Axel got on his phone, and no lie, about twenty seconds later the house was crawling with cops, all wearing their ten-gallon hats, handkerchiefs around their necks and long black coats.

They looked kinda liked fake leather, something I like to call pleather.

Officer Todd took Gilda away in handcuffs. The whole time she was whimpering, "Honey, you don't understand. I wasn't trying to hurt Sprinkles. I was trying to save her."

Likely story.

Once Gilda was taken care of, Officer Todd approached me. Sprinkles had dug a spot into the hollow of my armpit and was purring softly.

"Animal cruelty is a serious crime in Magnolia Cove," he said.

I nodded. "That's what Axel said. I'm glad we caught Gilda before she was able to do any harm to the cat."

Todd nodded. His gaze landed on Sprinkles before drifting back up to my eyes. "I'm hoping she'll admit to more than the potential abuse."

My eyes flared. "You mean like Ebenezer's murder?"

Todd pinched his fingers over the lip of his hat. "Exactly. I'm hoping she'll show us where she hid the will as well."

"You think she knows."

"I'm sure of it. But we've got her in custody now, so that's good news for you."

I cocked my head. "Good news for me?"

He flashed me a genuine smile. "Absolutely. This should absolve you of the crime. It means you're a free woman. You can leave Magnolia Cove."

My heart swelled. Free. I could go. Leave. Be gone from this place full of witches.

At the same time my heart sank. I'd only just found this place, this new family. But still, hadn't I wanted to go? Wasn't that my goal from the moment I found myself trapped here?

To get back to my old life, my own life.

A life that was crumbling faster than you could say *peach cobbler*?

I forced a smile to my face. "Thank you. I appreciate it."

"You're welcome." Todd reached out a hand, stroked Sprinkles.

At his touch the cat bolted up. She glanced back. When her gaze met Todd's, she leaped from my arms, claws wild. Sprinkles slashed a gash across Todd's cheek.

He lurched back. "Stupid cat," he said.

I watched her sprint off toward Axel. She jumped into the private detective's arms. He scooped her up and shot me a questioning look.

I turned back to Todd. "I'm so sorry. I don't know what got into her. She's never done anything like that before."

He yanked the handkerchief from around his neck and dabbed his cheek. "It's fine. Cats don't like me. Not sure why." His gaze flickered back to me, and he pushed a smile to his face. "Anyway, you, Pepper Dunn, are free to leave Magnolia Cove."

I bit my lip and watched him walk away. I inhaled a deep shot of air and thought, okay, all I had to do was get my car, go and have a plan for evading Rufus for the rest of my life. Betty could do the cloaking spell she had mentioned, and I could train myself on my powers, my head witch powers. I'd used the power a few times already; I could probably figure out the rest on my own.

It sounded like a relatively solid plan.

First thing tomorrow I'd be heading home.

TWENTY-TWO

Sweetie Death Wish—I mean Sprinkles—sat between Axel and me on the ride back to my house.

"Todd said I can leave town. He seems to think he can get Gilda to confess to Ebenezer's murder and also confess what she did with the will."

Axel's brow lifted. "All good. I can help you get past Rufus, if you like. I can direct you to others like us who can assist you, teach you so that whenever he shows up, you can take care of him."

I should've been grateful. Should've felt relief.

"Thing is…" I swiveled in the bucket seat so that one knee was hiked up as I turned to face him.

Axel tipped his head toward me. My chest bloomed. My heart pounded. Boy, what this guy did to me.

Course, we both had issues and had confessed that it wasn't the right time for us.

But slap me stupid, had his lips felt good on mine.

"What's the thing?" he said.

"So, you know my dad died a few years ago. I never knew my mom since she passed in childbirth. After he died, I squirreled away my feelings, picked emotionally distant guys to have as boyfriends. When

I look back, I realize that I didn't want to put myself in a situation where I could get hurt again. Being hurt is no fun. When I came here, I was wild-eyed and naive. I thought this whole witch business was crazy."

I sighed, rested my head back on the seat. "But my family—they've accepted me with open arms. Betty might be nuts, but she's my grandma. Cordelia and Amelia have both been awesome—they've helped me so much. Made me clothes, helped me with my first riding skillet. I don't know…"

Axel took my hand. He pulled over outside my house and pivoted toward me. "You know, sometimes caring for people can bring hurt. I know that. You know that. But often the rewards outweigh those risks. Your family loves you. They accept you. That's something, in my opinion, to grab ahold of and cherish above all else. Because we're brought into this world with only our family around us, and when we leave, that's who's hopefully there as well. Now we can't choose what sort of crazy we're born into. If it's bad, we make our own families. But Pepper, you've got one knock-down-drag-out gangbusters of a house full of women in there, and I think you know it."

I squeezed his hand. "Thank you. You've helped clear everything up."

And he had. My heart ballooned as I realized this was the place I was supposed to be. Not Nashville. Not anywhere else but Magnolia Cove.

I smiled.

Axel smiled, his dimple peeking. He dipped his head, and his lips brushed mine. Our mouths lingered. It was short and sweet, and when we pulled away, I cleared my throat.

"But that doesn't mean anything," I said.

He shook his head. "Nothing. Not a thing."

Then our gazes met, and we burst into laughter.

"But seriously," I said.

He nodded. "We've each got our own issues to work out."

I sighed. "So it doesn't mean anything."

He shook his head sadly. "It can't."

Axel opened my door. I hopped out with Sprinkles in my arms. A wind kicked up and Sprinkles jumped from my arms, scampering down the street.

I shot Axel a tired look. "I'll go get her. Thanks for dropping me off."

His brows quirked. "You sure?"

I nodded. "It's fine. Thanks for everything." I laughed. "As long as I'm back at the house before curfew, it should be fine."

"Okay. Call me if you need anything."

I smiled. "I don't have your number."

My phone buzzed in my purse. Axel grinned. "You do now."

"Impressive." We waved goodbye, and I set off after Sprinkles. She sat outside Betty's picket gate. But as I neared, she scurried off down the street, heading back toward downtown.

"Great," I mumbled.

Axel's taillights faded in the distance, and I hugged my arms as I strode through the quiet streets. One thing I had to say about Magnolia Cove, once darkness hit, the place got quiet fast. The few restaurants opened at night had a steady population of diners floating in and out, but the rest of the town hunkered down and faded into silence.

Sprinkles stopped outside my store. "All right, cat. Come on now. Time to go home."

But just as I reached her, she ran back off, winding around to the alley. I followed her to the back door of the pawnshop.

"Please don't run off again. I'm getting tired." But she didn't. Sprinkles jumped onto a low window and scratched at it. I reached for her, but she dodged my grasp. Again, pawing at the glass.

"Okay, what's this about?" I pushed on the pane, and low and behold, the window slid open. Sprinkles jumped inside. She popped her head back out.

"Follow," she said.

A shiver raced down my spine. She'd finally spoken. At long last, the cat had talked to me.

I studied the window. Now, with a little bit of Crisco and one good shove to my rear, I'd slide on through no problem. But I did not have Crisco, nor did I want to rub it over my naked body.

Now, if Axel was involved, that might be another story.

Wait. Stop that.

Focus.

As it was, I found an empty crate and stood on it. It was rickety, but it gave me enough height to get a good way into the window. I leaned up and over. My foot slid. The crate wobbled, slipping out from under my foot.

I pitched forward and tumbled inside, catching myself before I cracked my head on the floor. A wedge of pain lodged in my hip.

Groaning, I rubbed my back and side, working the kink out. I flipped a switch. The hallway lights glowed warmly, illuminating part of the shop in front. Sprinkles had jumped onto a bookcase and was clawing at one of the ancient tomes.

"What are you doing?" I said.

"Here," she said.

Her words fired crisp in my head. Why the heck hadn't she talked earlier?

I walked over to her. Her claw had snagged on a book. It looked like she was trying to pull it out. I hooked a finger on the top of it and yanked.

The book tumbled to the floor. "Oops. I guess I don't know my own strength."

The cover peeled back, revealing cut-out pages. A square of book had been dug out, creating a space to hide things.

"What's this?" I said.

My phone buzzed. I pulled it from my purse and checked.

It's me, Axel. Gilda had a heart attack on the way to the police station. They don't know if she's going to make it.

Ouch. Wow. Maybe the guilt had gotten to her.

I tucked the phone back into my purse and inspected the book. A folded sheet of paper had been tucked inside. Two folded sheets.

I opened the first one and started reading. It was Ebenezer's first will, the one that named Gilda as beneficiary. The kids were completely cut out of this one, and if Gilda died, it named Todd as the next in line to inherit.

I unfolded another sheet, and this one was the will everyone was looking for. Dean and his sister were the inheritors with Gilda as third in line. Todd was nowhere to be seen in this will at all.

A slow, terrible realization started to sink in. Cold, nasty fear gripped my heart and squeezed to bursting.

I picked up my phone, scrambled to retrieve Axel's number. I got it dialed.

"Hey, there. Miss me already?" he cooed.

"Axel, Gilda's not the killer. In fact, I think someone deliberately hurt her."

"What do you mean?"

"I found the will."

A hand yanked the phone from my ear. I whirled around to see Todd looming behind me. He threw my phone to the ground and crunched it beneath his foot.

I backed up. "Oh, wow," I said. "It was you. All along it was you."

Todd's handsome features twisted into a dark, serpentine look. He flicked a bit of dirt out from under his fingernails. "You know, I really tried to pin this one on you. I was going to be the hero, you see. I'd killed Ebenezer and then returned to the shop to be the sad nephew who found his uncle in a pool of blood. But then you came along and made it almost too easy. With blood all over your hands, how could you not have been the killer?"

He kicked my phone down the hallway, far from my reach. "But then everyone turned out to like you. The town embraced their new owner of Familiar Place. Didn't matter. The police would find the guilty party eventually. Of course, I still had one problem. I needed to secure the newest will and get rid of it. You've done that for me now, haven't you?"

He opened his palm. My grip on the paper tightened. His skin became dark, wraithlike. "Hand it to me before I suck the life from you."

"It was you. You're the wraith."

A slow smile curved on his lips. "One and only."

I pieced it together quickly. "Let me guess—your gambling bills became too much."

Todd nodded. "I needed that money to pay off Bubbles, but my uncle wouldn't give it to me. We struggled; the rest is oh so cliché. I killed him. He'd just changed his will, cutting me out of it completely. I managed to steal the lawyer's copy before it could be read—yes, that was me, too. Now all I needed was to produce the one that came before it. Get the older will to be accepted as Ebenezer's last will and testament and get rid of Gilda."

His gaze flickered around the room. "I also needed to get rid of the cat. Gilda was trying to do a protection spell on the animal tonight. That's what she was doing when you found her." He laughed. "She wasn't hurting it. She was protecting the stupid thing."

"So you attacked me at Gilda's house as the wraith. I'm assuming that was you, too."

"I was after the cat. And that stupid piece of paper you found? It was a recipe for her prize-winning pie."

I nearly planted a facepalm on my forehead. How stupid I had been. I glanced at the will. "So now you plan on destroying the true will, producing the older one for all the world to see and taking the money."

"I've got plans that include me, tropical women, fruity drinks and tiki huts. Once this will appears on the lawyer's desk, Gilda will be dead and I'll be named heir. And it's all thanks to you. I couldn't have done it without you." His lips twitched. "Don't worry. When I'm lying on the beach surrounded by my millions, I'll have a drink to your cold, dead body."

Oh wow. So that's where this was headed?

I shook out my hands. "Listen, I'm not going to tell anyone. You don't have to kill me. Seriously. Who would believe me, anyway? I'm not very good at witchcraft, I don't even really like animals, and I'm new in town. All things that mean no one will pay the slightest bit of attention to me."

Todd reached out a hand. Black, ghostly flesh washed up to his shoulder. Ew. I didn't know if that was permanent, but part of me wondered if his skin would get frozen that way. You know, like when you stuck your tongue at someone when you were a kid and your mom told you that your face would freeze that way.

I wondered if that's what would happen to Officer Todd.

I wedged my back into the bookcase. "I'm not going to tell anyone."

"It's too late for that," Todd said. "Much, much too late. Accept that you're going to die."

He reached out. Cold fear gripped me. I was struck dumb, paralyzed. Part of me thought it was Todd more than my own fear pinning me to the spot.

From behind me, Sprinkles hissed and launched herself at him. I heard her faintly yell, "Run."

The cat's claws raked over Todd's face. He cursed and lifted his arms, giving me the moment I needed. I raced down the hall, flipped the lock and fled out the back door.

I didn't know how long the cat could keep him occupied, but I had a feeling she had a world full of hate for him since he'd killed her master.

I sprinted down the street, not sure exactly where I was going.

Wait.

I did know where I was headed.

I would go home. To Betty's house. Surely she'd be sitting in the living room, shotgun in her lap. She'd be stocked, loaded and ready for action.

I only needed Todd to follow me into the house.

My thighs burned as I pushed myself fast down the road. I rounded off the main street, sweeping past rows of houses. I saw Betty's house just up ahead. It was so close. All I had to do was launch myself inside.

My foot was about to hit the front step, when—

Something grabbed a fistful of my hair. I was yanked back, landing flat on the concrete.

Pain arched up my back. The air punched from me. I gasped to fill my lungs, ease the pain.

Todd loomed overhead. He walked around, coming to stand at my feet. The detective made a motion of zipping a finger over his mouth.

I heaved a breath and tried to shout, but no sound came out.

He leaned down, filling my view with his wild, crazed eyes. "You can't speak. No one can hear you. It's sad, really, that your dead body will be found here, but there's nothing I can do about that."

His body darkened. His arms transformed into ghostly whips. Black fumes drifted off him. In a few seconds he would be a wraith and I would be dead.

I tried to get up, but it was no use. He was using another paralyzing spell on me.

Todd's face twisted into a sick, perverted look of victory. He lashed out. I shut my eyes, waiting for the worst.

Then a screech squeaked from his throat.

I looked up to see the guard-vine wrapped around Todd's neck. His fingers, now flesh, clawed at the vegetation, but it held strong.

The spell on me broke. I scooted back. I trained my gaze on Todd as the vine strangled the life out of him. It didn't release its hold until Todd's eyes closed and he sank to the ground.

The front door opened, and Betty stepped out. She gripped her shotgun hard as she took one look at Todd's lifeless body.

"Told you it was a guard-vine. You can never tell what kind of baddies are around. It's always good to have one." Her gaze drifted toward me. "Time to call the cops. Looks like Officer Todd is dead."

I rose on shaky legs and walked to the body. I reached trembling fingers toward his neck. There was no pulse.

Betty was right.

Officer Todd was quite dead.

TWENTY-THREE

*A*xel arrived about the same time as the police. I was worried that no one would believe me, that Todd had attacked me, but they had evidence pointing to the fact that he'd slipped Gilda a potion to make her have the heart attack.

Thank goodness, because I had been worried that I'd be arrested for Todd's death.

Axel handed me a warm Styrofoam cup. "Once they start digging, I think they'll find everything they need to know about Todd."

I sniffed the container. Hot chocolate. I licked my lips and pulled jelly beans from my pocket. Yep, I'd started stuffing them in pockets everywhere I went. I slid a few in the cup. "I thought I was dead, for sure. But that whole wraith thing, was that part of his magic?"

"It was," Betty said, striding forward. "As a policeman, he wasn't allowed to use it for his own personal gain, but he didn't play by the rules."

"There are some interesting creatures here in Magnolia Cove," I said to Betty.

"Tell me about it," Axel murmured.

I sipped the liquid. Warm chocolaty goodness with a hint of cinnamon slid down my throat. A thought hit me, and I bolted upright. "Has anyone seen Sprinkles? If it wasn't for her and the guard-vine, I'd definitely be dead. She attacked Todd in the pawnshop. Oh, and I think they'll find both wills on Todd's body, including the one naming Ebenezer's children as beneficiaries."

Axel rubbed my shoulder. "Calm down, there. All will be revealed." He picked a cat up from the ground and set Sprinkles in my lap.

I shot him a grateful smile. "Thank you." I rubbed the cat behind the ear and said, "Why didn't you tell us from the beginning it was Todd? You knew, didn't you?"

The feline rubbed her face against my hand. "Too hard to talk about it."

I hugged her close and glanced at Axel. "She says it was too hard to talk about."

He nodded. "The trauma of it. You know, she and Gilda might make a good pair. Once Gilda gets out of the hospital, you could pair these two together, now that we know she wasn't trying to hurt the cat."

I picked Sprinkles up so that we were eye to eye. "Would you like that? Would you like to live with Gilda?"

In response, the cat purred even louder.

I took that as a yes.

∽

A FEW DAYS later I sat down to breakfast with what I now considered to be my family.

Yes, family.

Cordelia, Amelia and Betty squabbled over who was going to get the last biscuit until Betty finally flashed a butter knife and threatened to give both of my cousins boils on their bottoms unless they let her have it.

After all, she said, she was the one who had cooked it. Not them.

The old lady had a point.

Me? I was settling into my life in Magnolia Cove nicely. I had ordered a few more animals to take the place of the ones I'd sold, and my allergies were dying down.

I guess it was simply being near the critters that had helped me out there.

I still saw Axel around, but we'd come to an understanding about things between us. There was no *us*, which, as much as he made me hot in lots of places, I realized was for the best. After all, I was now a businesswoman, and I needed to figure all that out.

And no, I hadn't tried to leave Magnolia Cove since the very first day I arrived. I knew Rufus was out there, waiting for me, and I didn't know what he wanted.

I planned to keep it that way—at least until I was powerful enough to defend myself.

I was locking up Familiar Place one Wednesday evening. The heat of summer was beginning to wind away, retreating, as cooler winds were whisking in at night.

"Hey there," came a gruff, husky voice.

I dropped the golden key in my pocket and glanced up. Axel leaned on the side of his Mustang. "Hey, yourself."

His dark hair was pulled back, and his blue eyes sparkled as the sun began to set. "Haven't seen you in a while."

I slowly walked over. "I've been busy. Running a shop. You've got my number." I fished my phone from my purse. I'd replaced it after Todd smashed the old one. "New phone but same number."

He nodded. "I've been on a case that took me out of town."

"Oh? I hope you solved it." A strand of honey-crimson hair fell into my eyes. I brushed it away. Axel's gaze never left mine.

He nodded. "I did… I thought you might like to go for a ride."

I grazed a hand over the glossy car. "In this? Is it a full moon tonight? Too bad it's not a convertible."

Axel's gaze sharpened. "No. It's not tonight. Not for another week."

I quirked a brow. "You know an awful lot about moon cycles."

"I have to."

"What?"

He shook his head. "Never mind. So what do you say? Want to go for a ride?"

I hugged my purse to me as I watched him. We'd built up trust, shared secrets. My heart pounded as his gaze met mine, and a tornado of chickens fluttered in my stomach.

"Okay," I murmured. "But it doesn't mean anything."

He crossed to me and opened my door. "Nope. Not a thing."

"Just have me back before Betty unloads a wad of buckshot into your rear end."

Axel laughed. "Promise."

EPILOGUE

"Dinner's ready," Betty yelled from downstairs.

I eyed Mattie on the window seat. "You ready for some chow?"

The cat made a chewing face. "It's Thursday. Chicken-and-dressing day. You bet yer underpants I am."

We went downstairs. Cordelia and Amelia were already at the table. Betty was dishing up the plates.

I impulsively reached out and hugged Betty.

"What's that for?" she said.

I shrugged. "It's for everything."

It was. My life had completely changed in the past few weeks, and in a great way. My grandmother deserved a thousand hugs for everything she'd done for me.

When the four of us were settled, Betty started scrolling through the list of eligible bachelors for Amelia, who rolled her eyes just about every other second while Cordelia checked the mail.

"We got a postcard from our moms," she said, lifting a square of paper.

Amelia took the opportunity to disengage from a man who

claimed to be the world record holder with his ability to create structures from paper clips.

Wow. Talk about boring.

Amelia's eyes flared. "Oh? What does it say?"

As Cordelia read, she choked on her dressing. I slapped her back until the food dislodged from her throat.

"That bad, huh?" Amelia said.

Cordelia's eyes were full of tears—probably from the choking episode—and said, "It's horrible. They're coming home."

I quirked a brow. "Who?"

"Our moms," Cordelia said.

"Oh good. I get to meet my aunts."

Amelia shook her head. "Oh no, this is not good. Not good at all."

"Why not?"

Cordelia passed the postcard to Amelia. "Last time they were here, they set half the town on fire."

"Oh no," I said. "Was anyone hurt?"

Amelia shook her head. "No. Thank goodness. No one was hurt. Oh no. It looks like they're bringing something with them."

"What?" I said.

Amelia raked her fingers down her face. "Some sort of magical creature they found in Peru."

Betty laughed. "They might raise the town right off its foundation."

"Sounds like fun," I said.

Cordelia shook her head. "No. It's not fun. They come in. They cause mayhem. They're generally incredibly disruptive. That's why we bought them the world cruise in the first place."

Amelia nodded. "They cause serious problems. And of course, they're going to want to meet you."

Cordelia nodded. "Just wait. They're going to try to get you to help them with all the bad stuff they do."

I pushed a green bean around my plate. "So what you're saying is—"

Betty snorted. "Your aunts are going to make you their partner in crime."

I lifted my glass of sweet tea in the air. "Well, if it's between causing havoc in Magnolia Cove or meeting up with Rufus outside it, I'll take havoc any day."

Cordelia raised her glass. "I'll raise my glass to that. To the sweet tea witches!"

Amelia laughed. "Sweet tea witches, I love that."

Betty laughed. "Y'all may be the first sweet tea witches I ever met."

"But hopefully not the last," I said, laughing.

The front door blew open. Magic curled in the air, sending sprays and wisps winding around the furniture.

Amelia rose, knocking back her chair.

Two figures stood in the frame. Both had long red hair, though one was completely straight and the other hung in loose, floating waves.

The women wore fur coats, heavy gold jewelry and enough makeup for a tribe of children to play in.

"Mom," Amelia said, her eyes shining with fear.

"Oh no," Cordelia said.

One of the women cackled and threw up her hands. Lightning flashed outside, sending a crack splintering the air behind them. "We're home!"

So I could see.

<<<<>>>>

ALSO BY AMY BOYLES

SWEET TEA WICH MYSTERIES
SOUTHERN MAGIC
SOUTHERN SPELLS

BLESS YOUR WITCH SERIES
SCARED WITCHLESS
KISS MY WITCH
QUEEN WITCH
QUIT YOUR WITCHIN'
FOR WITCH'S SAKE
DON'T GIVE A WITCH
WITCH MY GRITS
FRIED GREEN WITCH
SOUTHERN WITCHING

SOUTHERN SINGLE MOM PARANORMAL MYSTERIES
The Witch's Handbook to Hunting Vampires
The Witch's Handbook to Catching Werewolves
The Witch's Handbook to Trapping Demons

ABOUT THE AUTHOR

Amy Boyles grew up reading Judy Blume and Christopher Pike. Somehow, the combination of coming of age books and teenage murder mysteries made her want to be a writer. After graduating college at DePauw University, she spent some time living in Chicago, Louisville, and New York before settling back in the South. Now, she spends her time chasing two toddlers while trying to stir up trouble in Silver Springs, Alabama, the fictional town where Dylan Apel and her sisters are trying to master witchcraft, tame their crazy relatives, and juggle their love lives. She loves to hear from readers! You can email her at amy@amyboylesauthor.com.

Connect with me online!

amyboylesauthor.com
amy@amyboylesauthor.com

Printed in Great Britain
by Amazon